Ancient Water

*A Water Chronicle Featuring
Dr. Francis Allenton*

Dennis Edwards

Plain View Press
P. O. 42255
Austin, TX 78704

plainviewpress.net
sbright1@austin.rr.com
1-512-440-7139

Cover Art: *The Birth of Water*, © Amanda Edwards, 2006.

Acknowledgments

I wish to express here my gratitude to

my wife Pam for her continued help editing and, as always, her voice of encouragement and reason;

my friends Jim Walker and Rose Keene for their reviews and Rose's precise proofreading;

my sister Nancy Eaker for her technical expertise concerning laboratory procedures;

my cousin and friend Larry Smallie, who tells me that he remains astonished at my attempts to fill the world with new ideas.

Chapter 1
Water Cartel Office

Alford Purlough stood to speak. The twenty high-ranking members of the Water Cartel had gathered for their quarterly briefing. As he stood in front of them, he felt a weakness growing in his legs. Suddenly, a powerful, invisible force caught him just behind his knees causing his legs to buckle. As he started to fall he grabbed the podium.

Holding on tightly, he drew a deep breath and murmured, "Late night, excuse me, ladies and gentlemen."

Alford gathered his scattered files and arranged them back in order. He knew it was risky to appear weak in front of people with such power. Gathering his strength and clearing his throat, he began his report.

"The water project with the military sector has gone very well. Over three hundred thousand bottles of water are being consumed per day by our troops. The insurgency and civilians in both Iraq and Afghanistan are consuming twice that amount. The hostile acts on both sides continue and our long-range forecasters predict at least three and possibly five more years of conflict in the region. When hostilities cease, we will continue to control the domestic water production. We are projecting twenty billion dollars per year from this area.

"We are currently beginning to shift our focus to water production in Europe and China. Our initial figures are very promising. I would like to spend a few moments to bring some of our newer members up to speed with our latest interests."

"Before we move to the future, Mister Purlough, I was wondering if you could clear up a few lingering questions?" A thin figure stood. He had been hired less than two years ago but had risen in the ranks of the Cartel quickly. Alford disliked the young man's thuggish nature and suspected he was driven by nothing other than his own ambition.

The weakness returned to Purlough's legs. He held onto the podium trying to mask increasing sensations of pain.

"Certainly, Adam." Purlough was aware he pushed the name out through his lips the way one would push out a sour grape.

"It's this Lin business and the missing doctor." Adam responded.

"Go on."

"Lin was terminated?"

"Yes."

"Under whose authority?"

"Perhaps, Adam, since you are new to the organization, you need to know that it would be more prudent to ask such questions where we have a greater degree of privacy. Not everyone assembled here needs or wants this information."

"I have information that Doctor Allenton and his new bride have fled the country. He seems to be searching for his missing Caduceus."

"We have all read the same report, Adam." Purlough said trying to sound more polite than caustic.

"Would it not have been prudent to have completed the cleansing of people involved in this project?" Adam asked.

Purlough took a deep, audible breath, "Doctor Allenton posed no threat to the project. His reputation was dubious at best when I recruited him to complete work on the aggression formula. Although he was totally unaware of our goal, he did exactly as we hoped. He confirmed that the soluble minerals in the bottled water would produce aggression yet not be detected. We had no need to undergo the further expense of termination. He posed no continuing threat to our plans. Lin, on the other hand, had made contacts outside the Cartel with his homeland. In all likelihood he never quit working for China."

"The report does not resolve the issue of the missing Caduceus." Adam pressed Purlough.

"We believe the Caduceus was hidden by Lin, but he was killed prematurely before we could destroy it. However, it was simply a canard, a ruse with which to recruit Doctor Allenton. No one believed it had curative powers. We allowed its construction to keep his interest, and after we had the aggression formula, neither the Caduceus nor Doctor Allenton were important to us."

"He is in France now." Adam revealed to the Cartel members.

"Yes, Adam, he is there doing research under a grant we funded to get him out of the country. He is doing research on ancient springs."

"He is dangerously close to our continuing operations in Evian."

"He represents no threat to our operations. We have neutralized a number of our past employees by giving them employment within the Cartel's extensive system under our management. It is far better to keep them idle in our system than let them roam the world and stumble into problems from which none of us can benefit. Historically, the Cartel's policy is to take terminal action only on rare occasions. Customarily we employ scientists at various projects around the globe in our shadow corporations. This keeps them in our sights if we need to use them again."

"Yet, Allenton is close to our European Space Agency plan as well."

"A mere coincidence, I can assure you." Purlough had begun to feel nauseous. "If there isn't anything else then?" He attempted to end his part of the meeting. He was feeling clammy and looked down at his colorless hands.

"Are you quite all right?" Adam asked.

"Perfectly fine." Purlough answered. He tried to hold onto the podium but fell to the floor, unconscious.

Chapter 2
Control room, European Space Agency, Paris

The rocket began to move toward its strategic position. Earlier that month it had been sitting on the surface of a comet. The series of feats had seemed improbable: track a comet, fire a probe to its surface, melt the surface ice, and gather the melted water into a container designed to keep it in liquid form. Then, launch the protected container from the comet to be recovered by the mothership. Yet, all of these had been accomplished.

The public had only been told that the ship had crashed on the surface of the comet and in so doing, it was able to make a number of precise measurements concerning the make-up of the comet. Well-positioned members of the Water Cartel had directed the European Space Agency's plan to recover stellar water. These scientists knew the blast of the rocket would be detected on Earth, so the cover story of a crash landing was developed. The real plan, however, was to recover stellar water.

For decades these powerful men had known that transporting sustainable water to colonize space was too heavy and too costly. Water had to be found among the stars. They believed that water from the beginning of time, probably the same water that seeded the Earth with vast oceans, had the potential for immense commercial profits. No one knew for certain just where liquid water would be found in space. Even if it were in space, no one knew if it would be the same as water on Earth. However, the Cartel members believed that if man were to explore the heavens, a source of potable water had to be found. They intended to be the first to establish the rights and technology to harvest the water of space.

"She's coming around." The technician told the flight manager. "Twenty seconds to fire the braking sequence."

"Do we have a go?" the manager asked.

"Go."

A message was sent by microwave to the rocket. Engines fired and the craft rotated and slowed. The door on the ship's side opened to robotically collect stellar water and deposit it in a container to be securely locked in a protective chamber. A constant temperature would be maintained to insure that the stellar water would remain liquefied, neither freezing in space nor evaporating during re-entry. A second blast sent the stellar water traveling toward the Earth as the ship flew above the atmosphere.

"We have disengagement." The technician said. "Trajectory looks good."

“Deploy chutes.” The manager ordered.

“Deployment sequence valid. Chute deployed. Trajectory nominal.”

“Recover the container.” The manager turned and walked toward a telephone.

“Purlough here.” The voice on the other end answered.

“Baby is delivered.” The man said softly.

“Splendid.” Purlough tried to say, but could only cough. Recovering his voice, he spoke, “Excuse me. Splendid. Well done.”

Chapter 3
Rural, dusty field, Texas, USA

Seven young boys were playing basketball. They were so absorbed in the play of the game that they did not notice a streak in the sky above them. A meteorite had traveled through space like an arrow shot toward a round, moving target. It had neither wavered nor decelerated since being blown from space debris by a collision with another meteorite. Within the center of the Earth-bound meteorite were purple crystals. Within those crystals rested the most important substance of the universe: liquid water that had formed at least three billion years ago. The secret cargo was encapsulated in the meteorite's cover of stone that had been made smooth by the journey.

"Ball hog. Pass it over," Mark yelled in his youthful Texas drawl.

"Hey, look at that, a falling star." A boy behind him pointed toward the sky.

The boy with the ball took advantage of the distraction to throw the ball into the net, but it swished through without notice. A sonic boom had interrupted the peaceful afternoon followed by a whine, increasingly shrill, signaling that the meteorite was speeding toward the ball field. The atmosphere exploded again with a boom and a tremor as the meteorite struck the ground.

"It's a freaking UFO!" one shouted. The boys raced to the house closest to the ball field.

"Mom! Mom!" Mark yelled. "It's a UFO."

"What's that, honey?" his mother said turning from the sink and drying her hands.

"A bomb or something just fell out of the sky."

"Mark, I'm busy just now."

"Mom, really. Come on, take a look. I'm not lyin'."

She looked out the window at a large smoldering, depression in the ground. "Don't you boys dare go outside. I'm calling 911." Mark's mother said.

Within hours the object had passed from the local police to an information officer at the nearby Houston Space Center. The boys went back to their basketball game that afternoon avoiding the nearby depression that was roped with yellow tape. Mark's mother watched the newspaper for an article. None appeared.

Only a few scientists at Houston were privy to the details of the discovery. In a quarantine room, standing behind a protective shield, they opened the meteorite to find purple, sodium chloride crystals. Liquid water lay inside the crystals exactly where the hands of time had placed it.

Chapter 4
Paris, three weeks later

The knock was unexpected. Cassidy hesitantly moved toward the door. Francis and she had been living in Paris for less than a year. She still struggled with her meager facility of the French language and strangers at the door put her into a panic.

Cassidy pulled the door open until the chain caught. She could see a man smiling as he stood outside in a suit and tie.

"Yes?" she asked.

"Madame Allenton?"

"Yes. I am Cassidy Allenton. May I help you?"

"I am Maurice Flauneau of the European Space Agency."

"European Space Agency?"

"Most certainly, Madame Allenton. I wish to speak to Professor Allenton. It is of the utmost urgency."

Cautiously, Cassidy let her eyes roll over him. She was not comfortable with living abroad and had only agreed to move to Paris to be with Francis.

"Doctor Allenton is not home at the moment."

"It is most urgent that I talk with him. May I wait for him?"

"Inside?"

"Well, that is customary."

"It might be customary where you come from, but I'm from America and we keep strangers on the other side of the door."

"How long will he be?"

Cassidy wondered if the truth was wise. Francis was not expected until late that evening, but she didn't want the man on the stoop to know she would be alone most of the day.

"I'm expecting him shortly," she lied.

"Shortly? Excuse me, but I'm not certain I understand your meaning."

"Shortly. You know, directly."

"You mean soon?"

"I mean directly. You'll have to call back later. I'm going to be going out soon."

"Meaning directly?"

"Yes. I'll be going out to do my shopping directly, soon."

"May I leave my card?"

She had begun to close the door.

The man started to put a small business card through the open space toward Cassidy. "A moment more, if you please." Flauneau pleaded. "I have been a fan of your husband's work for years. I have read everything he has ever written. His reputation as a water scientist stretched across the Atlantic. I was thrilled to learn of his arrival in Paris to work on the primitive water study. What I have to tell him is exciting news. He will want to hear it."

He dropped the card and it fluttered down coming to rest on Cassidy's right foot. She closed the door and then stooped to pick it up. She felt he was still standing right outside. She had learned that the French were nothing if not persistent.

"I'll tell him." She yelled through the door. The apartment was small with a bay window that offered a view of the stoop from inside the house. Cassidy inched close to the edge of the bay window's brocade curtains and peeked out at Flauneau.

He spoke to her as if she were on the other side of the door. "He will be very disappointed with you for not inviting me in. Yes, Dr. Allenton will be very disappointed."

"I'll tell him." She called to him.

"Very well then, Madame, I will wait to hear from him." Flauneau said. Cassidy watched as he went down the steps, got into an old Peugeot, and drove away.

She sank into the divan and breathed a deep sigh of relief. At least he had spoken English. She was not at all comfortable with the French language. Her decision to come to Paris to be with Francis was a monumental event in her life. Francis had pleaded with her before their marriage to try living in France for a year, and then, if she could not adjust, he would try to obtain a research position back in the United States.

She knew he needed to find his Caduceus, the copper device he had finally created only to have it stolen along with all of his lab equipment. They were certain that when she drank the spring water spiraled through the Caduceus, she had been cured of breast cancer. They also had many reasons to believe that the Water Cartel and Alford Purlough had stolen both the Caduceus and Francis' reputation.

Primarily Cassidy had agreed to leave the States because they both suspected that Dr. Lin, Francis' research partner, had been murdered. The official report had said Lin died in a random robbery and mugging, but they were convinced he had been killed for what he knew. Lin had worked for the Cartel but, unlike Francis, probably knew that the Cartel's goal was to alter bottled spring water to produce aggression in government and the troops. No one they talked to in Washington admitted that a

Water Cartel existed, especially one that was powerful enough to affect global politics.

Francis continued to be obsessed with finding the Caduceus. He knew that Lin had it after it was stolen and before he died. After Francis traced Lin's family to France, he accepted employment in Paris as a water scientist hoping to find the missing device. Living near the ancient springs in France also allowed Francis to learn more about the world of bottled water and the Water Cartel's interests and investments in Europe.

Cassidy was proud of her moving to France. She struggled to learn French but simply did not have Francis' affinity for languages. Sometimes she felt she knew just enough to get herself in trouble, but in spite of the struggle with the language, she admired the Parisians' passion for life. The intensity of the Europeans resonated deeply within her. She disliked the superficial Midwest American politeness often presented when the situation clearly called for dissent. Cassidy liked a good sparring but in Paris felt at a distinct disadvantage when the conversation slipped into French and she could not express herself.

Francis had a strong command of French and would often end up talking for her. She hated the way that made her feel dependent on him. Today her shopping list consisted of a loaf of bread, some wine, cheese and a software program she had located on the internet to help her learn French.

She decided to call Francis at work before she left.

"Doctor Allenton." His voice both soothed and aroused her.

"Doctor, would you mind coming home and giving me an injection?" her voice was deliberately low and sexy.

"Who is this?" Francis teased.

"Shut up."

"Hey, sweetheart, are you all right?"

"Some guy nearly beat down the door looking for you. He's your number one fan in France."

"Who?"

"He stuffed his card through the door. Martin Flauneau. He said it like we would say, 'I have the flu now'."

"Flauneau? With the ESA?"

"The what?"

"European Space Agency."

"Europe really does have a rocket ship?"

"Yes and flush toilets. Come on, Cassidy, you know they put a space probe up last year?"

"Yes, I guess I remember that.

"Yes, we talked about their probe into deep space."

"So what does this have to do with Flauneau?"

"The probe was looking for water."

"In space?"

"It happens that there is a lot of water in space, sweetheart."

"Water in space? Is that what makes the rain?" She sometimes feigned ignorance to lighten him up.

"Okay, Cass, water in space does not make the rain."

"I guess I should tell you that Flauneau said you would be disappointed in me for not letting him in."

"Did he say what he wanted?"

"No. He said you would want to know about it."

"Did you?"

"What?"

"Did you let him in then?"

"No! I'm not letting a stranger in."

"Give me his number then, would you?"

"Yes, but, Francis, are you going to be late again tonight?"

"No, well, unless something comes up."

"Like our first date in Eureka Springs?"

"No. Hey, I thought you forgave me for that?"

"Well, you did marry me. I guess that should show your intentions were honorable."

Cassidy gave him the number and hung up. She recalled the first time she met Francis in Eureka Springs. She was a hospice nurse in nearby Southwest Missouri. He was a presenter at a conference on aging that she was attending. They met in the hotel hallway when Cassidy ran from a ghost in her room. Eventually he had confided to Cassidy that he was really in Eureka Springs to get a sample of spring water that might have curative capabilities. She felt comforted remembering the beginnings of her romance with Francis and the first spring water she drank. Time had carried them forward, but sometimes she thought they were still in the early stages of their relationship.

Cassidy sighed and let go of her reverie. She donned a hat and large dark glasses so she could avoid eye contact or be forced into conversation while shopping.

Francis called Flauneau and a secretary put him through.

"My God, it's good to have you call, Doctor Allenton."

"Just call me Francis."

"I wouldn't dare." Flauneau said as if some social breach had occurred.

"Can I help you, Mister Flauneau?"

"Yes. It's wonderful. We have water."

"Pardon?"

"The probe we sent to Enceladus has come back to us."

"That's not possible. I read that it crashed on the surface."

"This is what we have told the public."

"And?"

"It was designed to return a sample."

"What sample?"

"Primitive, ancient water. Water from the dawn of time."

"This is not possible."

"So we thought, but none the less, here it is. We also have a sample from the Texas incident."

"I would give a year's pay to examine it, Mister Flauneau, a year's pay."

"I thought you would be interested. I'm your greatest fan. I've read everything you have ever written."

"Can I see it?"

"It's going to be difficult. We have partners that are most anxious to see it as well."

"How difficult?"

"Very!"

"So, why are you calling me?"

"In Paris the difficult can sometimes happen. You have an expertise I need. In fact, I think you may be the person most prepared in the entire world to examine this sample. There was one other man, an Asian man, but he is dead now."

"Can we meet?"

"Certainly. But it must be soon. That is why I came to your house."

"Name the place and the time."

"Tonight. I'll call you back. Thank you, Doctor Allenton."

Francis stood thinking then dialed home. "Honey, I'm going to be home really late."

Chapter 5
Water Cartel Office

The long range planning group for the Water Cartel had begun its meeting. Adam was leading the proceedings.

"Mister Purlough sends his regrets, ladies and gentlemen. It seems he has fallen ill. Let me assure you that I am well-briefed on the latest direction of the Cartel and can lead the discussion."

"What is the latest on the space probe?" one of the members asked.

"We have been successful in the recovery of the stellar water. As it now stands we will begin analysis immediately to determine the nature and structure of the water. We have gathered one of the top teams in France. They are working diligently but, of course, unaware of our involvement and financing."

"Could you remind us, Mister, uh, I'm not sure I know your last name." a woman at the end of the table addressed him.

"Halter, Adam Halter."

"Could you review for us, Mister Halter, this project's parameters?"

"Under deep cover we have funded the recovery of stellar water from the Cassini project. The close fly-by planned for Enceladus will deploy a gathering device. That device will be returned to our labs in secrecy. A portion of the returned water will be studied to determine if it is liquid water, the same water as found on Earth."

"To what purpose?" the women asked again. Adam's forehead developed a deep frown suggesting irritation with her failure to remember the previous explanations given by him two months ago.

"If space travel is to be undertaken, the provision of potable water for the journey is a major obstacle. Water weighs nearly ten pounds per gallon and the only other option, the distinctly distasteful method of recycling water from human urine, really isn't feasible. However, water in space is an absolute necessity for extended travel and colonization. Therefore, we diligently strive to answer two questions: is water available in space, and if available, is it the same liquid water found on Earth. If it is, we will be the first to franchise the mechanisms of production, control, purification and distribution. Our right to franchise water in space has been confirmed by our lawyers and their interpretation of the Space Exploration Treaty passed by the U.N.

"There may be other applications for this water as well. We do not know the chemical composition of stellar water. Some have suggested that it is closer to heavy water and therefore toxic for human consumption. However, others say it may possess curative powers for a variety of problems that have beset our planet. Whatever the outcome, the Cartel intends to tie up the rights to stellar water."

"Are we solid with the people on the project in France?" a voice asked. "We don't want any more of those problems with personnel."

"We have several well-placed people on the project. I myself intend to take Mister Purlough's place and attend the analysis. I will be leaving tomorrow."

"Is Purlough seriously ill?" another voice asked.

"I'm uncertain of his current status, but let me assure you this project is in my hands. Nothing will slip by me." Adam both glorified his own capacity and impugned Purlough in the same sentence. He knew that several in the planning group blamed Purlough for Lin's indiscretions.

"Mister Purlough has served us long and well." a voice gave support.

"Let the young man feel his wings." Another voice gave Adam support.

"Thank you, General." Adam gave a look of appreciation to his sponsor. The General and Adam's father were chums. Adam had been raised to believe that wealth walks down the same corridors of power. His father frequently reminded Adam that in all significant groups, no one stands alone at the top. No talent rises to the top without invisible hands of support. Those hands expect special favors and thus, loyalty propels people forward, not because of expertise, but because of favors owed and debts paid.

Adam continued, "I can assure you, nothing like the embarrassments that arose in the last project will occur under my watchful eye. We shall never have a problem with the likes of Doctor Francis Allenton."

Adam finished his briefing, outlining the possible benefits of stellar water's use in a number of projects. He was satisfied that he had aroused doubts about Purlough's past leadership and created his chance to flourish.

A continent away, Francis returned home after a late night meeting with Flauneau. After letting himself in the door as quietly as possible, he checked his wristwatch. It was nearly two a.m. He slipped off his shoes and crept toward the kitchen avoiding the spaces in the old floor that he knew would always creak loudly. The round-topped refrigerator shuddered as the motor shut off. The long chrome handle reflected the light from a streetlamp outside the kitchen window. He was hungry.

"Tramp!"

"Zeezus H Christ!" he said as he turned to see Cassidy standing behind him. "Don't you ever sleep?"

"Not when you are out late. How did it go?"

"Interesting."

"How so? You want something to eat?"

"Yes. I'm starved."

"We have cheeses, grapes, some meat and bread."

"Whatever. They want me to look at something special."

Cassidy flowed toward him in her favorite long nightgown, the one he said she floated in since it was so long it hid her feet. She saw him watching her and nudged him out of the way toward a chair at the small, wooden table they shared for every meal.

"So?" Cassidy turned the conversation back toward his meeting.

"So, it was interesting. What do you know about space?"

"You mean that big wasteland of emptiness with stars in between?"

"That's the common idea — that nothing's out there, but in fact, the whole universe is full of things we can't even imagine."

"Green men? UFO's? Like that?"

"Perhaps, but I'm speaking of more simple things. Water, hydrogen, carbon, the building blocks of life spread from end to end of the universe."

"Cheese?"

"There's no cheese, silly!"

"No, you dumb cluck, I mean do you want some cheese?"

"Oh. Yes, thank you, sorry."

Cassidy gave him one of her tolerant smiles. She knew the universe wasn't full of green men, UFO's or cheese. Francis always took things too literally when he was serious, and once he was locked on to an idea in the conversation, he could not seem to defocus his attention long enough to conduct the daily requirements for living. He often forgot to eat or would fall asleep at his laptop. Cassidy liked to tease him back into contact with her. She wondered at times if she didn't find a way to gather his attention, if Francis would end up an isolated, dirty-shirted geek. Still, she thought him adorable when he got lost in thoughts too deep to easily recover.

"Interesting?" she steered him back to the meeting again.

"Yes. Intensely. You remember Cassini?"

"Certainly. He designs expensive clothes." She gave him one of her smiles.

"The Cassini space probe. You know about this. We talked about this not long ago."

"Yes, Francis. I recall the space probe. It was going into deep space to get a close look at some of the outer planets."

"Right, right." Francis looked at the plate of carefully aligned slices of meat and cheese and fruit and the hunk of crusty bread. Cassidy might be having trouble with the language, but she had quickly adopted the

European-style presentation of food. "The ESA has a probe going out as well. It's called the Rosetta probe."

"As in the Rosetta stone?"

"Yes, exactly like that. I think they named it the Rosetta Probe because like the Rosetta stone they hoped it would unlock all kinds of secrets. One of the goals of the project is to launch a probe that will land on the comet."

Cassidy smiled and started humming "Catch a Falling Star and Put It in Your Pocket."

Francis raised his eyebrows but continued eating.

"Comets are made of water vapor and stones, aren't they?" she asked.

"Yes. Well, some are, and the one they are chasing is thought to be made of water, ice to be more precise. The comet's name is Wirtanin. They are going to fly very close to the comet for a while and then land on it and drill into the ice."

"What are they hoping to find?"

"It's more what they are hoping to learn. They want to analyze the ice and determine if the frozen water is the same water that we find here on Earth. It's a puzzle really."

"The comet?"

"No. The puzzle is the origin of water on Earth."

Cassidy sat down across from him and leaned forward. "Tell me more." She loved to listen to him even in the early morning hours. He was a deep thinker and when he wanted to explain something complex, he always rubbed the space between his eyes for a minute or two to gather his thoughts. Now as she waited, he rubbed between his eyes.

"Well, five thousand million years ago the water on the Earth was formed. Some say by the hand or will of God and others say by more scientific processes. What is clear, from recent studies in space, is that water vapor results as stars form. It has to do with the collision of atoms of hydrogen and oxygen and stellar forces, but it seems indisputable that water is widely distributed across the known and unknown universe."

"So water in space."

"Not only water, but lots of water in the form of ice. Some of the moons around Jupiter, for instance, are nothing but frozen worlds of ice. The polar caps of Mars and our own Moon seem to have water below the surface. Recent detections from a special project of the ESA, the ISO it is called, found water vapor widely spread in the universe and in particular around newly formed stars."

"ISO?"

"Infrared Space Observation, it's a way of looking at the stars for specific elements. Well, they found water vapor almost everywhere they looked."

"So the poets were right about sailing the heavens."

"Ah, yes, technically I guess." Francis seemed to be considering what Cassidy had said.

She waited for him to continue, then teased, "Some water scientist would love to find out about this water from the heavens, wouldn't he? Who's the clever boy?" Cassidy smiled at him as she tilted her head while shifting her weight from side to side.

"Yes, I'm the water scientist, of course. God, I would love to see some of that water under a microscope. There can't be any more primitive water than this water. Geez, my first project was water from deep wells in Europe deposited probably six or seven thousand years ago. Then I looked at the deep core samples from Antarctica. The water at the poles was formed perhaps fifty thousand years ago and that ancient water has profoundly interesting aspects for us to study. But, Cass, what if I could get a sample of water from hundreds or perhaps thousands of millions of years ago?"

"Can you?"

"I might be able to look at a sample. The Cassini probe isn't due to fly by the Earth until 2017, but Flauneau says he has extraterrestrial water. He says I might have a chance to look at some of the water that was found recently in a meteorite that fell to Earth right next to some kids playing basketball in America."

"Did anyone get hurt?"

"No. But when the scientists split open the meteorite, it had crystals and, to everyone's amazement, water. One of the crystals contained liquid water. You can't imagine how impossible that is."

"So, you might get a look at it?"

"Flauneau says I might. He can arrange it."

"Why?"

"Why what?"

"Why would he let you look at it?"

"He knows my reputation."

"I'm sorry, Sweetheart, but you remember the last time we got mixed up with the water people."

"Yes."

"Francis, that other scientist, Dr. Lin, was killed, and Purlough and the Water Cartel ruined your reputation in America, and here we are in Paris to be safe, and your Caduceus might be hidden somewhere here and — "

"Cassidy, this is nothing like all of that."

"Francis, beware Greeks bearing gifts of water."

"Funny, funny."

"Francis, consider this, there must be about two drops of water on Earth from stellar sources and Flauneau wants you to look at it. Doesn't that seem, well, interesting?"

"He knows my work and I still have a reputation and respect here."

"So that explains everything then, doesn't it."

"He has more water for me to see."

"From where?"

"From space."

Cassidy saw the pleased look on Francis' face, but she wasn't ready to let go. "From space, how?"

"Don't know."

"Don't know?"

"No."

"Hon, please be careful."

Chapter 6

The next morning at breakfast Francis was bustling about getting dressed and ready to go. Cassidy was a slow riser. She awakened and shuffled her feet into the kitchen area where she brewed strong French coffee. Even though her hair was scattered all over like the papers on Francis' desk, she looked beautiful to Francis. He managed to make a "Chuck, chuck," noise with his cheeks and lifted his eyebrows at her.

Cassidy smiled broadly at his flirtation then slowly sat down in an over-stuffed chair balancing her coffee cup carefully. "Still riled up about the space water?"

"I've been thinking about Halley's Comet."

"That's what I like about you. You think of nothing but me in the morning." She blew on the top of her coffee.

"Halley's Comet had a close fly-by a few years ago. Giotto made close contact in March of 1986. It got within 200 kilometers of the comet and was able to take readings of its core."

"Giotto?"

"A space probe from the ESA named after Giotto di Bondone. He had observed Halley's Comet in 1301 and did a famous painting of the Star of Bethlehem using the comet as the model. Well, anyway, the Giotto found the comet's core was active, still spewing out energy. They had always thought it was active and full of volatiles."

"Volatile gas?"

"Well, yes and no. Volatiles in space could be water and that's exactly what they found. The composition of the comet's tail revealed over 80% water. Of course, there were other elements like carbon monoxide, methane and ammonia, but by and large, it was water. Analysis showed the comet had formed 4.5 billion years ago from ice that had condensed onto interstellar dust particles."

"Now that's some old water." Cassidy remarked as she took her first sip of coffee. "It's nice being married to someone who thinks something four and a half billion years old is interesting. I'm not a bit worried about growing old with you." She made a puckered up face at him.

"Well, that's not the interesting part. I think they may have recovered some of the material. Giotto was programmed to have a near Earth fly-by, and I heard rumors that it had the capacity to return the samples to Earth in a special pod that was to jettison as it passed close to the Earth."

"Do you think Flauneau knows about it?"

"I think he is connected to the project. He works with Philae."

"Who?"

"No, Philae is a what, the planned probe that intends to land and take core samples from another comet. If I'm right, and I think I am, these people have been returning samples of comet material, chiefly water, for the last ten years. I've been wondering why a space scientist would have read all of my articles on the effects and properties of primitive water. If they have ancient water, water from the time when the universe was formed, they would be deeply interested in my view of its properties."

"So, Francis, we know of three probes: the Giotto in 1986 and now the Cassini and the Rosetta all seeking stellar water. Okay, different groups are looking for water, but isn't water, well, basically just water? H_2O?"

"Yes, that's right, but then again it might not be just plain old water, but water whose basic structures might contain amazing properties. What if I can expand my work on the restorative and curative nature of water that has been spiraled? If the spring water is curative, especially if spiraled in the Caduceus, then what properties might stellar water have?"

For a moment Cassidy envisioned the tall metal and stone Caduceus that Francis had built. They believed that spring water spiraled through that Caduceus had cured Cassidy of breast cancer. "So, Francis, you think this ancient stellar water could also be healing?"

"More than healing, it may contain the very stuff from which life on Earth developed. In particular, it may contain a form of hydrogen we call heavy hydrogen as compared to the more common form of hydrogen found in Earth's water. Comets and everything out in space should be made from the same materials. If there is a different kind of material in ancient water, then we would have to look to an external explanation of how it got that way. How was it modified or how did our water modify itself after it was seeded on Earth? Perhaps the explanation lies in an extra solar origin, a source different than the source that produced our water on Earth."

"Francis, religious people would tell you that the origin was God. The ancients believed that rain was the blood of Gaia."

"I'm aware of these two very different opinions. Some believe that the originator of all life was not of this Earth while others contend that life is self-generating coming from the Earth Herself or Gaia. For me, there's an extraterrestrial explanation. However, if the ancient water is exactly the same as Earth's water, then that is an equally fantastic discovery because the thing that is holding back space exploration is man's dependency on water. If water is everywhere in the universe, then man can go there and harvest the water vapor and turn it into potable water to drink and use. Perhaps liquid water is in space as well, perhaps beneath the surface of frozen planets or under their poles. If water is spread across the cosmos, then so is life."

"So, it's very possible that water is everywhere in the known universe."

"Yes, but we don't know what kind of water it is, what its properties are. Perhaps there is water, water, everywhere and not a thing to drink."

Cassidy giggled, "Sorry, but talking about all this water, makes me have to go tinkle."

Francis began rummaging through the papers in his office. The phone rang.

"Got it!" Francis called out to Cassidy.

He picked up the phone, "Hello!"

"Doctor Allenton, this is Maurice Flauneau."

"Yes. Good morning."

"Can you meet with me today?"

"Certainly."

"I'll come by and pick you up in say, half an hour."

"That will be fine."

Francis rummaged again until he retrieved the study he was looking for in his office. Cassidy emerged from the bathroom. She raised her eyebrows in a manner to suggest she wondered who called.

"Flauneau. He wants to meet with me this morning."

"Do be careful, Francis. I have a funny feeling about this. Investigating healing water with others brought you trouble back home."

Francis dressed, took his briefcase and placed it near the front door. He paced until a car pulled in front of the house. Flauneau emerged, and as he approached the front door, Francis came out. "Good Morning, Flauneau."

"Yes, Doctor Allenton. It is a pleasure to see you again. Are you ready to go?"

"Where are we going?"

"My office at the E. S. A."

Flauneau drove with abandonment. He was obviously excited and as soon as they pulled away from the curb started telling Francis what they were going to do. Whenever he spoke, he looked at Francis and drove across the center line. More than once an oncoming car honked and people shook their fists at him out their windows.

When he looked at his passenger and said, "Francis, it's pre-biotic," he took a turn a little wide scraping the outside of the curb with his tires. At the same time the engine of the car made a hissing sound.

Francis was holding the door handle tightly. "You mean, no sign of organic life? How do you know?"

"The first sample arrived over ten years ago."

"I suspected as much. Was it from Cassini?"

"Yes. The comet was composed of ice crystals and we got a good sample on the close fly-by."

As Francis thought about this information, the car screeched to a stop and Flauneau turned off the motor. The car ran on in protest. Francis presumed the engine oil had never been changed and thought perhaps at any moment the motor would fall out from beneath the hood. Flauneau locked the doors and left the car shuddering in a parking place. As they approached the elevator, Francis heard the car let out one more very loud clang and then die. Flauneau didn't seem to notice.

Francis resumed their conversation. "So the water is pre-biotic. What did you do when you obtained the first sample?"

"Of course it was under strict containment. We didn't want to unleash a plague upon the Earth from whatever the water might contain, but under examination it contained nothing. No life whatsoever of any type. No DNA could be found. However, there were some structures we could not identify. It was pure water."

"What of the hydrogen molecules?" Francis was intent on Flauneau's answer.

"That's another matter. What do you suspect?"

"Heavy!"

"Exactly. I knew you were the right man. Let's go in."

The laboratory was guarded heavily. Francis had to sign some forms and Flauneau talked to the security chief. After a blazing argument, Flauneau prevailed and Francis was admitted. The chief of security glared at him as he walked past with a visitor's badge pinned to his shirt.

The laboratory was in cramped quarters, typically European and Spartan, but efficiently supplied. The lights gave off a buzzing noise. Men and women worked in cubicles and paid no attention to Francis and Flauneau as they walked past.

"Why the security?" Francis asked Flauneau.

"Why? You have no idea what people will do to get the information we have."

"I might have more ideas about people than you think." Francis thought of the last time he worked on a water project.

Flauneau entered numbers on a pass key security device and they entered a completely enclosed cubicle. "The sample I want you to see is fantastic. We had precious little water in the first place. Some of the experiments have resulted in sample loss, but we have enough." Flauneau directed Francis to a microscope.

"Is it biotic at all?" Francis asked.

"No indication of life whatsoever."

"It doesn't answer the question then, does it?" Francis asked. "I mean, if the water is devoid of any kind of life, non-biotic in nature, then how did the water on Earth give rise to life on Earth?"

"I was hoping you might develop a theory about that when you have looked at it. Although it is non-biotic, it seems to have a capacity to, well, let's wait and see what you say."

Flauneau fumbled for some keys and unlocked a door in a large locker-like closet. He removed a set of slides from a temperature and humidity controlled vault. He eased the glass slides into the mount of an extremely powerful microscope.

Francis slid forward on a small stool with casters that squealed in protest. He took off his glasses and adjusted the microscope and sat in dead silence for a few moments. Suddenly he pushed himself away from the microscope and fixed his eyes on Flauneau.

"What are those structures?"

"We don't know. They have been tested for DNA and there is none."

"None?"

"Exactly. There is no indication at all. Isn't it fantastic?"

"Well, yes and no." Francis was perplexed.

"Say again!"

"I anticipated something, anything. This is the stellar water?"

"Exactly."

"So, why exactly do you need my expertise?"

"It's not what the water has in it that I wanted you to see. It's what the water does when introduced to water that does have microscopic life in it. That's the puzzle."

"What does it do?"

"Take a look."

Flauneau produced a second slide. He pushed the sample under the microscope and Francis slid forward again.

"Wheeyou!" Francis said under his breath.

Flauneau moved closer. "You see, Doctor Allenton?"

"Yes, I see."

"Life. Life everywhere in abundance. Life and primitive forms not seen on the Earth for millions, perhaps billions of years."

"You added the stellar water to sea water and it produced this explosion of life?"

"Yes."

"So when stellar water is introduced into the ocean water, this happens. How?"

"That's the question I want you to answer."

"Where did the ocean water come from?" Francis continued without looking up from the eye piece.

"The Baltic Sea. It's just simple sea water carefully collected in sterile sample bottles some time ago. Tell me, Doctor Allenton, what do you know about heavy water?"

"I'm not an authority on it."

"You are falsely modest, Doctor Allenton, I have read your papers."

Francis sat up straight, put on his glasses, and spoke softly, "Well, heavy water is present in ordinary water in a ratio of one to seven thousand. It can be created using chemical and physical processes, but it is expensive. The number one producer is Canada. It's a by-product of their production of nuclear electricity. They have made heavy water commercially available."

Flauneau said nothing so Francis continued, "As you know heavy water is also called deuterium water and should be considered toxic for human consumption because it seems to displace light water and disturb the rate of biochemical reactions in the body. Its chemical description is D_2O as opposed to H_2O. This simply means the nucleus of the deuterium has one proton and one neutron whereas normal hydrogen has just one proton. Thus, it causes, or is more easily used, to cause a nuclear chain reaction."

"As you said, you don't know a lot on the topic." Flauneau's tone was teasing. Francis' knowledge of the subject was obvious.

"I think the Noble Prize in 1934 was on this topic. Isn't that right?" Having experienced a loss of credibility as a scientist in the United States, Francis sounded pleased to be respected again.

"As you say." Flauneau was impressed.

"Of course, heavy water was a concern in World War II with the Germans trying to make the first nuclear weapon. But, for the most part, weapons now rely on enriched uranium or plutonium more than heavy water."

"This sample of ancient water has the characteristics of heavy water."

"Have you used it in non-saline water?"

"Yes. The same. Less dramatic, results. There was rapid development of biotic life, but not to the same extent as the sea water."

Flauneau reached over and made an adjustment on the microscope while he spoke, "The Monahan's meteorite, the one from Texas, was encased in salt crystals. Isn't that right?"

"Yes, purple salt crystals about 3 millimeters long. Why, what are you thinking?"

"Maurice, I'm thinking there is a connection. The question, as I see it, is twofold: where did all the water in the Earth's oceans originate, and what lead to the profusion of life in those oceans? The first thing that occurs to me is that the oceans are full of salts. The importance of salt relates to the collection of neutrinos. Salt is used in neutrino collection systems. The sodium chloride seems to attract bombarding neutrons and when they collide, they produce heavy water. We know that heavy water is mutagenic."

Francis took off his glasses and rubbed the skin between his eyes. He turned to face Flauneau and said, "Thus, if what is happening right now on this slide mimics what happened as the Earth's oceans were seeded, the Cambrian Explosion may be explained. It could be that comets with high collections of salts brought ancient water to the Earth. If the ancient water was neutrino rich, and if the Earth's waters at that time were pre-biotic, full of life's potentials, then the combinations would have spurred rapid development as well as spontaneous adaptations which some call evolution."

"Doctor Allenton, you do not disappoint me. Now, what do you know of the dead zones?" Flauneau asked.

"Very little." Francis replied. "On the increase, aren't they?"

"Yes, dead zones in our oceans are rapidly increasing. Perhaps as many as 150 zones are now confirmed across the world. Mostly they are found where major water ways of industrial countries empty into the sea. The process is fairly direct. Excessive nutrients from farming or industrialization flow both treated and untreated into the bay. The nutrients are fed upon by the phytoplankton. The richness of the food source leads to a plankton population explosion and the seas become dense and block the sun light from the sea floor or upper areas of the water. The life that feeds upon the plankton is suddenly in a situation where the oxygen is depleted by the large plankton population and thus, these predatory vertebrates die. When they die, they sink to the ocean floor where disposers of the flesh digest them and create a kind of black scum on the floor of the ocean. These areas are essentially devoid of life, dead zones."

"You are talking about areas like the Gulf Coast in America." Francis stated.

"Yes. Dead zones in America, China, Europe and Asia are all expanding. You remember the second slide you saw, the one with all the biotic life expanding?"

"Yes."

"One of the things missing on that slide was plankton. The new forms of life feed on the plankton."

"I see!"

"If we could introduce a large quantity of extraterrestrial water and re-produce the conditions under which sea life exploded, we could eliminate the dead zones in our oceans by releasing these predators. They would feed on the plankton. The waters would clear and the ecological system would be back in balance."

"Human engineered bio-technology to correct the dead zones, it's provocative."

"Perhaps we could revitalize the oceans. Think of the implications. We could demonstrate the resurgence of the Cambrian era. We could prove that stellar water arrived on Earth, filled the seas with life and caused that life to mutate."

"The great flood." Francis said as if it were obvious.

"Yes. I have considered that a meteorite primarily composed of water might have saturated the Earth with extraterrestrial water. This would have produced a tremendous amount of heavy water and perhaps given rise to the explosion of life on Earth. This is even more likely with a neutrino storm from the sun to energize the oceans."

"We are off into extreme speculation, Flauneau. I usually like to work in the world of explanation. Yet, still, as a hypothesis, it is provocative."

"The water sample from the meteorite in Texas has the capacity to provoke an explosion of life in our sample of sea water. The next step is to see what happens if it is introduced into a sample of water from a dead zone with extreme populations of phytoplankton. If the predators emerge and eat the plankton, the seas will clear."

"Perhaps, Maurice, but only in a very controlled setting." Francis' voice changed from high and excited to tense and firm.

"Yes, of course, Francis. We would not risk putting this process in place on a larger scale until we know the outcome."

Flauneau moved away from the microscope and poured himself some bottled water. "Would you care for some, Doctor?"

"No. I've had a bad experience with bottled water. Thank you all the same."

"I am prepared, Doctor Allenton, to offer you an opportunity to be part of this research."

"How so?"

"We have approached our founders and they have authorized me to bring on whomever I need as principal investigator of the stellar water. I know of no one with whom I would prefer to work."

"I'm flattered. I'll have to take it into consideration."

"I need to know today."

"Today?"

"We are leaving within the week to collect samples from the dead zones and I want you to be part of the process. Are you interested?"

"I'm interested, but I have a partner."

"Yes, I've met her."

The telephone in the ESA security office rang. "Yes?" the Chief of Security answered.

"Did you admit a Doctor Allenton into the center?" Adam Halter asked.

"I did. He was a guest of the director." The Chief replied.

"I don't want that man anywhere near this project."

"What's that?" Alford Purlough spoke from behind Adam. "Who are you talking to, Adam?"

"France, sir." Adam resented the intrusion, but Purlough had seniority in the Cartel.

"A problem?" Purlough asked.

"Nothing I can't handle while I'm over there." Adam returned his attention to the phone and the Security Chief, "Do nothing until I arrive."

Leaving the room Adam met the General as he went toward the elevator.

"The plan is in place?" the General asked, looking side to side to insure no one was listening.

"Yes. Release of the heavy water into the number twelve water feed system in Quebec. There are a number of people of all ages. There are a few schools, a nursing home, and a neighborhood. All and all a wide spectrum of subjects will be exposed."

"Do we have medical personnel on the payroll?"

"Yes. Everything is in place for the test."

"What do we expect?" the General strode to the window and looked out at people walking beneath him.

"We expect wide spread symptoms. Children and elderly will be most affected. The heavy water will be introduced to determine the health reactions. We have medical personnel with our serum and others with a placebo."

"Deniability is in place."

"It can never be traced to our source in Canada. The supplier has been terminated as a precaution."

"Very well. You have my order to proceed."

"One more thing, General."

"What?"

"Allenton has shown up at the ESA lab. The stellar water project director invited him into the project. Security picked him up on our profile list."

"How the hell did that happen?"

"Too much latitude given to the project director by Purlough."

"We are beginning to see Mister Purlough as a liability."

"I am aware. Steps are being taken. He is too well-placed to be eliminated by conventional means. I will be on a plane to France tomorrow."

"Keep me apprised. I don't want any events to get in the way of the stellar project. Too much is riding on this. If our Canadian project is going to be successful, we can't afford Allenton snooping around. How in the hell?"

"Flauneau did not know of the past difficulties."

"Adam, you are paid to prevent this type of thing from happening."

"I'll be there tomorrow, General."

"Then handle it, Mister Halter, handle it."

Chapter 7

Francis talked very little on the way home. His mind was swimming with the possibilities with stellar water. Flauneau let him off in front of his apartment and gave him a slow and knowing nod as he left. They had arranged to talk by telephone that evening. Flauneau wanted an answer.

Cassidy was in the bathroom when he came through the front door. "Be out in a second." She yelled. The door latch made a loud click and she emerged looking pale.

"You all right, Sugar?" Francis asked.

"Yeah. Been on my knees all morning."

"Sorry I missed it. You got religion?"

"I got pregnant."

"What?"

"Yep. Even in French the easy home pregnancy test kit says we hit a homer."

Francis stood silent. He searched Cassidy's face for some hint of an expression he could mimic. If she looked distressed, he was prepared to give comfort, and if she looked pleased, he was prepared to embrace her with joy. She showed nothing.

"That's a good thing, right?" Francis asked.

"Is it?"

"Well, hell's bells, yes."

"Whew, that's how I felt about it." Cassidy finally smiled broadly. They moved together and held each other for a moment. Then, stepping back a little, Francis touched her stomach gently. She smiled at him and put her hand over his.

"Cassidy, are you going to be all right, I mean, with your past history and all?"

"As far as I know, I'm perfectly fine."

"We are going to have to go back home. I mean, you can't have a baby over here."

"They have babies in France."

"I know, I know. It's just, well, we need to be sure everything is fine."

"Everything's fine, Francis. How was your day?"

"Not nearly as exciting as yours was, apparently."

"No, really. What's up?"

"It's not important. Not now."

"Of course it is. What happened?"

"Oh, I saw something amazing. Star water."

"And?"

"And it seems to spur biotic development."

"That's good?"

"It could save the Earth."

"That seems to be as important as my day."

Francis led her to the divan and they sat down still holding hands, "No. That was all speculation. This new life of ours, that's what's really happening. Having a baby isn't about theory and science."

"Save the Earth how?" Cassidy fixed her eyes on Francis.

"Well, the oceans of the Earth seem to be having a problem. Did you ever hear of dead zones?"

"Yes, remember I was an environmental activist in my college days. Your space water can fix them?"

"I'm not certain. Flauneau wants me to sign on and be part of the research. But, that is not as important as a baby."

"I don't want our baby to come into a dead world with dying seas and a sick environment. This is important, too, Francis."

"It means travel and being away from you. I don't think that is such a good idea, not now anyway."

"So when is it a good time for you to study this water?"

"Flauneau wants my answer tonight."

"What's the question?"

"There are a lot of questions."

"Is there a chance?"

"Yes. I think there is."

"I'm good with this, Francis. I'm open to this."

"We are still on our honeymoon. I don't relish the idea of being gone from you."

"Neither do I, Sweetheart, but this is a chance to do something for Mother Earth."

"Yes, that's true. But this is our chance to have a family and get that right as well."

"Don't be such a polar thinker. Maybe we can do both. I knew you were destined for greatness when I met you. This could be the moment you have trained for all your life. I'm not going to be selfish and stupid about it."

"Well, I'm not going to run off to all parts of the world and have you left here by yourself."

"We can talk about that part later. I want you to call Flauneau and tell him you're in."

"I don't know, Cassidy, I think — "

"Pick up the phone now before we both regret it for the rest of our lives."

Francis called Flauneau and agreed to be part of the project. Cassidy could hear the excitement in his voice as they talked. When he hung up his face seemed to beam.

"Where are you going and when?" Cassidy asked him.

"We fly tomorrow to the Baltic Sea and from there to America's Gulf Coast."

"Tomorrow! Why the Baltic?"

"The Eastern Baltic sea has a dead zone almost 100,000 square kilometers in size. We need to get samples from two areas in that zone. One from a limited area where there has been some revitalization. We want to take a look at how Mother Nature is correcting herself."

"What do you mean by revitalization?"

"It's a little complex, but at first it was so dead that an alien species, small jelly fish, was able to come in and take over."

"What happened then?"

"Well, oddly enough, larger jelly fish came and ate the smaller ones and that seems to have restored that part of the sea to an earlier healthy state, but there is another intervening variable." Francis stopped.

"And that is — " Cassidy gave him her sweet smile that meant Francis had stopped after using a term that really didn't explain enough.

"The intervening variable was the fall of Communism — it may be more responsible than Mother Nature."

"So, tell me the rest of the story."

"Well, when the Communist system fell, the government quit pouring tons of money and tons of nitrogen into the sea because they simply couldn't afford it. The farmers went back to the old ways of raising crops and thus very little nitrogen from the fertilizer ran off into the water in the sea and the plankton explosion couldn't be sustained, so the little jelly fish were eaten by the big ones and in that area some self-correction has occurred."

"So, using your logic the fall of Communism saved the Baltic Sea?"

"Well, sort of." Francis said in a furtive voice.

"Usually I'd put my money on Mother Nature. Leave her alone and she will fix herself."

"That may have been true once, a long time ago, but the world has grown too complex to let natural sources correct themselves."

"Not in the Baltic apparently."

"That is most likely an accident of nature."

"So all of Mother Nature's corrections must seem to man at the time they happen."

"Oh, Lord, Cassidy. Are you siding with Mother Nature? Next you'll say that the Earth is a living, sentient being."

"It's better than thinking she is a hunk of rock hurtling through the universe."

"The Earth is a hunk of rock and it is hurtling through the universe."

"At first glance it may seem only a rock, but if we look deeper she seems to be alive. I mean it is a living system, capable of repairing itself. If people take themselves off the Earth by some means, a million years or so down the road the Earth will become a harmonious environment again."

"If mankind destroys the Earth — "

"You presume mankind could destroy the Earth."

"I presume mankind has the destructive power to do so. I know it does."

"I think Mother Nature will find a way to get along just fine without mankind. Mankind is so arrogant thinking that Earth could not get along without us. Don't forget, Francis, I was actually an eco-extremist in college."

"Extremist?"

"Yes, we marched, we protested, we staged sit-ins. Even now you and I contribute to several of the projects."

"We do? Like what?"

"We send money to Save our Seas and the National Center for Ocean Science. I thought you approved. It's all about water, after all."

Francis put on a grumpy face. "How much do we give?"

"Oh, we are very generous. Perhaps they will throw a dinner for you when you go to the Gulf Coast."

"We give that much?"

"Well, maybe just a luncheon, certainly not a banquet."

Francis sat quietly for a few moments. Then he looked up and asked, "How was your research today?"

Cassidy spent many hours searching the internet for clues about the missing Caduceus. She also loved to gather information about strange anomalies of the Earth.

"The world is an odd place to live." She replied.

"The only one we have, so far."

"I saw a report on a skin disease that's becoming an issue for more and more people. There are lots of skin cancers out there, but this isn't. It's one I've heard of before — Multiple Chemical Sensitivity."

"Did you find anything on the Caduceus? Sooner or later, someone will do something that will give us a clue where it is. The Water Cartel, Lin's family, someone is bound to slip up and try to use it, alert some reporter, just do something that will attract attention."

"Actually, Francis, I found some stuff on Lin's family today. I'm sure there's more if I could read Mandarin. Some of the relatives may have a home in France near a small town on the German border. However, while that seems to be the area where some settled, there might be some family members still in Paris."

"Thanks, honey, I do appreciate how you keep searching for clues. Was there anything on water in the news?"

"Yes, a bunch of kids got quite sick in Quebec. They think it was some kind of problem with the water. They're trying to track it down."

"Quebec?"

"Yes. Does that mean something?"

"Well, maybe. They do make a lot of heavy water in Canada."

Chapter 8

Early the next morning Flauneau came to get Francis in a taxi. The journey from the Paris airport to their dead zone destination on the Baltic Sea was exhausting. They had to change planes in three airports and each time they endured an extensive search of their luggage and equipment. However, in spite of the difficulties, Francis soon learned that Flauneau was a good travel companion. He talked freely and with great passion about the state of the Earth's oceans and the prospects for the stellar water to rejuvenate the dead zones.

Flauneau was adamant that his research was going to save the dead zones. "Francis, curtailing agricultural runoff is a lost cause. Too much money is in it. People want their food, and they won't stand for reduced production. If we could get them to reduce the nitrate run off by forty or fifty percent, then it might make a difference, but people won't stand for it. The best approach is to attack the problem at the plankton level, or at the very least, the algae level. Perhaps we could even harvest the algae for other uses."

"It's the oxygen depletion, that is the problem, isn't it?" Francis asked.

"Yes, exactly. Fully oxygenated water has perhaps ten parts per million of oxygen. Once the level falls below five parts per million, large fish and other aquatic animals can't live. Sharks vacate the area if it falls below three parts per million and some fish and bottom dwellers can make it all the way down to two parts per million. It becomes hypoxic to sediment dwellers around 1.5 parts per million. That's the level of the dead zones."

"How long does it take for the hypoxia-fostered collapse to take place?"

"You ask a hard question. It varies by location, season of the year and other factors, but in some instances, it can go from a healthy sea to a dead zone in less than four years. No one listened to warnings in the Baltic a decade or so ago. Fishing was fantastic, but it was because the fish were too weak and too sick to migrate so the over- harvesting just made it all collapse sooner. I wanted us to visit the Baltic first because it is so devilishly hard to reverse the hypoxic collapse. I want you to see the microbiotic sea life in a revitalized dead zone. The Baltic is the best place."

"You said seasonal variations make a difference?"

"Yes, of course. The plankton thrive in the sun, but the winter causes the plankton blooms to perish or reverse. However, once the sun is in the summer sky, the blooms return."

"Your approach then would be to attack the dead zones by killing off the excessive plankton population that feeds on the nitrates."

"Yes, that seems the most realistic given that agriculture and existing practices are not likely to change. You know, Francis, people are reluctant to change practices when they can make a profit. The fertilizer companies are very wealthy and connected. It is not likely they will reduce the sale of their products and a hungry world won't stand by as supply goes down or prices increase. We have a chance to see this reversal in the Baltic because the Soviets quit spending money in the region. If we could attack the plankton in the winter, before they bloom, we could make a difference."

Francis quickly replied, "We do depend on the plankton for oxygen, I mean, the Earth depends on the plankton to produce a good portion of the oxygen we breathe. We could not afford to destroy the plankton totally."

"Yes, the plankton produces more oxygen than all the rain forests, so you are right, we cannot risk destroying the plankton. But plankton is one of those things that cuts a swath in two directions. Too many, we have dead zones, and too little, we have a dead Earth. The balance of plankton on the Earth is extremely important."

Both men were quiet. Francis was anxious to see the effects of natural revitalization in the Baltic. He found himself wondering if nature had found a way to self-correct, like the large jelly fish consuming the smaller ones, yet he had to take into account human action that might play a role as well as the change in farming methods that had reduced the nitrate emissions.

Francis did not know that Flauneau had larger demons: he had not been completely honest with Francis concerning the real intentions of his employers and the stellar water.

Chapter 9

"Mister Purlough, it's your son." The secretary's voice interrupted him.

Purlough disliked calls from his son at the office. He felt a close family was a liability.

"Yes?" Purlough's agitated voice greeted his son.

"Father, I have bad news."

"More financial problems?"

"No. I thought you would want to know this. It's Marilee. She's ill."

Purlough quickly switched his interest away from the report on his desk and the itching that had broken out on his arms.

"Is it serious?"

"Yes. It seems it is."

"Can I do anything?"

"No. Not just now. There is one thing."

"Yes?"

"Are you aware of anything going on up here in Quebec, I mean, are you aware of anything to do with the water?"

"Nothing. Why do you ask?"

"They say there might have been an accidental discharge of heavy water into the drinking system."

"Really. That seems impossible. They must be just casting stones. They can't really think heavy water has entered the system."

"Her symptoms are suggesting this. Hers and all the others."

"How many?"

"Six hundred. Some are old, some young, some middle-aged. The children and older folks are suffering the worst. The whole town has changed to bottled water. I just thought you might know something."

"Six hundred? No. No, I don't know anything. Can I call you back later?"

"Yes. We will be at the hospital. Use my cell phone number."

"I'll call, son. I'm sorry about the visit I'd planned, things came up."

"You know Marilee adores you."

"Yes, and I adore her."

"She did a report on you. They had an assignment for science. She was bragging about you. She told them you were trying to save the world by making the water clean."

"Did she?"

"Yes. I'm worried about her dad."

"She will be fine. Don't get shaky on me. I'll look into it."

Purlough rose from his desk and went to Adam's office remembering that he was on a flight to Europe. Purlough disliked Adam intensely. Every encounter Purlough had with him left him feeling that Adam was watching and reporting back to someone. Purlough found Adam's desk was locked as well as the safe.

Purlough had a key since it had been his office at one time. He tried it to no avail. The lock had been changed. Returning to his desk he called Eastland, a well-placed director in the Cartel who answered after the first ring.

"Eastland, Purlough here."

"Hello, Purlough, you old dog, we missed you at the briefing."

"I'm better now."

"Don't get sick on us, the other old dogs will eat you for breakfast."

"Got a question for you."

"Go."

"Quebec?"

"Under the radar."

"The General?"

"Who else?"

"Who's the point man?"

"Adam, who else but his ass-kissing protégé?"

"Where are the parameters of the intervention?" Purlough asked.

"Don't know."

Purlough immediately suspected this was a lie. Of all the members, Eastland would know the details of a release of heavy water into a drinking system. Purlough suspected the release was to test the responses to a specific amount of heavy water and document the result of serums that had been developed.

Purlough pushed. "Testing mortality?"

"Wouldn't know. It's all in the General's camp. He assured us it will be discrete, not more than a dozen would be seriously harmed. I need to go now." Eastland hung up the phone unaware that his answer had twisted like a knife in Purlough's gut.

Alford Purlough had a long history of doing things that hurt people. He had approved the murder of Lin and ruined Doctor Allenton's reputation. He had diverted millions of dollars away from projects that helped people into sleight of hand contracts that furthered the agenda of the Cartel. Now he found himself a part of something that had poisoned his granddaughter. He was sick. He knew the itching on his arms was a sign of a greater illness. The whole world seemed suddenly ugly and his world even more so.

He walked over to a window and stood watching several children playing in a park below. He considered his alternatives. While he was a wealthy man, few had been able to retire from the Cartel. Those that tired of the work were retained in honorary roles, received big pay, and saddled with the implicit promise of secrecy that tied them forever to the group. Purlough disliked being owned. He disliked even more that the ethics, such as they were, had slipped to such depths.

He examined his own heart, long encrusted and resonating to only the value of money. He found compassion for his granddaughter, but also hatred for Adam Halter.

He realized that some maladies were self-inflicted, therefore, they could be purged. Did he have enough time?

Chapter 10

Francis called home.

"Marci bon coup!" Cassidy answered the phone as if she had just failed French class in a Midwestern high school.

"Don't even." Francis said.

"Honey! How are you?"

"Tired as a dog with a steak tied to its tail."

"Oh, poor baby. How's your water?"

"Funny!"

"No, isn't that some kind of famous greeting?"

"Yes, that's right. How are you feeling? Have you felt anything, I mean, has little Francis done anything yet?"

"Yes, I think he is doing calculus."

"Did you go to the doctor?"

"Yes, it's official. I'm still a virgin."

"Get your money back. He's obviously a quack. Seriously now, what did he say?"

"He said to take it easy and ask my husband to do more around the house. I told him you were busy off saving the world and he told me to tell you to turn your attention to more serious issues."

"That's helpful. Did he actually say anything about the baby?"

"Yes. I'm probably a month and half along. I had to tell him when we conceived little Francis so I made up an outrageous story about you. It had to do with a trapeze set and a swing. He seemed impressed. You have a reputation in Paris now."

"Can't wait to get back and face the paparazzi. Now, seriously, did he say anything I should know?"

"He asked me out. You know how Doctors are, you being gone and all, me with my sparkling American mystique. Has Mother Nature impressed you in the Baltic?"

"I could say that she's nearly as pretty as you."

"Silver-tongued devil. Please go on."

"It's interesting. A lot of people are amazed about the area of reversal. It gives a lot of credibility to the self-correcting Mother Earth theory."

"Told ya so. Just leave Her alone and She can get the job done."

"We're taking samples from several areas for comparison with the Gulf of Mexico water. We're going there tomorrow."

"You're going to compare the regenerated water of the Baltic Sea to the Gulf that is still toxic?"

"Well, to be precise, it's not toxic, it is dead, but yes, I want to compare them for biotic life."

"I know someone there — in the Gulf area."

"Who?"

"David Pearl. We were in college and in the same Ecology Club. He went down there to study with some woman from the Louisiana Marine Institute or something like that. I think I have his number."

"You have his number?"

"He was a friend in college. Don't ask."

"Don't ask what?"

"You're asking!"

"Okay, fine. Give me his number."

"He's been mapping the dead zones in the Gulf for years. I remember when he went down there to study with the biologist. He quit school and stayed on. I think his number was on his Christmas card."

"Fine. You find it. I'll call him. Look, I've got to go now. Flauneau is outside and we have a lunch date."

"Call me tomorrow?" Francis' voice cheered her. She wanted him to know she was supporting his dream, but she missed him, too. "I wish I were with you." She added.

"Yeah, I know. I miss you, too."

"Well, yes, but sometimes I wish I were doing something as important as you are."

"You are, Cassidy. You definitely are. Anymore news of the kids and water?"

"Quebec, it seems, had heavy water in their drinking water."

"Impossible."

"So they thought. Poor people, it has really hit some of them hard. Couple of kids and elderly died."

"Wow. I'm sorry to hear that. Anything on the Caduceus?"

"Lin's family definitely has property in France, but Francis, listen to this, I might be getting closer. I sent an email to a group that claims it has evidence of a levitating Caduceus."

"Levitation?"

"Yeah, they say it jumps right off the table when they apply current."

"Print that out for me, will you?"

"Betcha bottom dollar."

"I'll call tomorrow."

"Love ya."

"Me, too."

Francis went outside and down the block to a small café. Flauneau was waiting at a table pouring himself a glass of bottled water.

"Careful with that stuff." Francis smiled at him.

"How is your lovely wife?" Flauneau asked.

"Pregnant, sassy, and smarter by accident than I'll ever be on purpose."

"Three blessings in one woman. It is good to have a woman with spirit, yes? Didn't you say she is a spiritualist or something like that?"

"Yes. She is a proponent of the Gaia Theory."

"An interesting match for a man of science."

"You are familiar with the ideas then?" Francis asked more to make conversation than challenge Flauneau's knowledge.

"Yes, it's Lovelock's theory. Basically stated he said the mass of all living matter on Earth, more strictly speaking the entire planet, functions as a vast organism that modifies its own environment to meet its needs."

"That's the basic argument. Do you agree?"

"I may surprise you, my new friend, in some areas I absolutely agree."

"For instance?"

"The notion of a reflexive, self-aware and self-regulating loop of behavior in any living system is well-known. The issues are the very definitions of what is alive."

"Let's accept that the Earth is living. Then what do you say to the idea that it knows on some level how to cure itself or make adaptations for its own benefit?"

"Francis, the idea that the Earth can be autopoietic, self-making, is an old idea and common to many cultures and their religions. Some things that occur on the Earth seem to confirm Lovelock's ideas. I'll give you an example."

"Fine. Let's hear it."

"The salinity of the sea is in a perfect balance with the creatures that live within it. This was first explained as a Darwinian by-product of natural selection that favored organisms that most matched the salinity, but the problem is how has the ocean managed to maintain a precise balance when the effects of erosion have pushed tons of salts into the sea? Yet we find the ocean and the creatures within it in a precise balance, one to the other. If it is the sea that has made the adaptation or the creatures is not important, what is important is the self-regulating process that maintains the balance. The slightest change in salinity, from three percent to four, would bring mass extinctions yet there is no fossil evidence of this happening. Even when you look at Earth-shaping events, the balance is maintained. How does it happen and who or what is regulating the process?"

Flauneau finished his statement and pushed himself away from the table. He seemed pleased with himself as Francis watched him. He folded his napkin and placed it on his lap, one hand smoothing it while the other folded.

Francis leaned forward. "Some would say life itself is regulating the processes on Earth with no more intentions than an amoeba would have. Lovelock said the Earth was a super-organism, but he stopped short of saying it was a living being."

"On the other hand, Francis, if the definition of life is a self-regulating organism, the Earth meets the conditions for a living entity."

"If we define life as a self-regulating set of processes." Francis countered.

"Many define life exactly that way even if there is no apparent intention or conscious to the activity, it is still life. Did life adapt to the conditions of the Earth or did the Earth make adaptations to allow life? That is the great question of this debate, Francis. It is the question of cause."

"So, Maurice, do you believe the Earth is a living thing?"

"In a short answer, yes, but what I believe is not the same as what science can prove. The problem with most human beings is they arrogantly believe that very little else on Earth is alive. When viewed from space and in comparison to our solar neighbors, the Earth seems very much alive. What do you believe, Francis?"

"I have not spent much time with my beliefs. I tend to spend more time with my observations and conclusions."

"Do you suggest that a conclusion is less than a belief?"

Francis sat back in his chair. It seemed that Flauneau had made a point that had escaped Francis' logic.

"It is an informed belief."

"And do you suppose that others come to their beliefs any differently than you?"

"I'm a scientist and that — "

"That means you have a fancy language and process to achieve your beliefs, that's all it means."

"Ideas that can be verified by other neutral observers. This is what science uses."

"We delude ourselves as much as an innocent child who listens to the preaching of his parents and decides to believe what he has been told. Eventually it all comes down to what you believe. For you it is the scientific methods and for others it is what their hearts tell them."

"You need to have a cup of coffee with my wife."

"I believe I would enjoy that."

Francis noticed the emphasis on the word believe.

Flauneau picked up his bottled water and poured the last remaining amount into his glass. "Some things are too small for us to examine and yet, they may be alive by the definition we are using. Other things are too large such as the Earth or universe, too large to use our methods of examination and determine if they are alive or if they are not. If they are alive, they live without any awareness of our ability to pronounce them so. When a person is dead, he has no need of a pathologist to pronounce him dead. When something is alive, it has no need of science to declare it to be alive. Life and all things living may take place on levels too large or too small for us to understand. The atom, the sub-atomic structures, one day may be found to be alive. The Earth, the universe, and all that we know even if beyond our comprehension, may be alive, alive in wonderful ways."

"Yes, Maurice, you and Cassidy should definitely get together."

Chapter 11

They rode quietly to the airport the next morning. The flight to New Orleans was less arduous with fewer stops than the trip to the Baltic, but Francis was tired when he arrived. He was greeted by hot and humid Gulf air laced with the smell of decay. A large billowing cloud lay off the shore and thunder could be heard as it made its way across the surface of the water. They settled in their accommodations that had long ago seen their heyday.

The morning sun found its way through a crack in the curtains and fell across Francis' face. He reached for Cassidy but touched only the empty bed. He realized that his tiredness had overtaken him the night before and he had failed to call her. He stood and stretched, his body aching from too little sleep trying to adjust to the passage through several time zones. He walked out on the balcony of his room wishing for a cup of morning coffee and looked at the bay. It seemed peaceful and in the distance he thought he could see dolphins playing at the water's surface. Small waves hit the sandy beach just beyond the hotel pool. The water in the long ago abandoned pool was rancid and full of palm leaves. The telephone rang. Francis stepped back into his room.

"Hello."

"Francis, this is Maurice. We have a ride coming after breakfast. We will be going several miles south of this location to gather our samples. Would you like to have breakfast together? We must go soon."

"Yes. That would be fine."

Across the street from the hotel was a small diner. Francis stumbled across the threshold and bumped a newspaper vending box. The souls of their feet made sounds like sliding sand paper on the floor. Many customers had carried sand from the beach and were probably used to the feel and sound of this beach front diner. Francis slid into a black vinyl booth seat across from Maurice.

"How did you sleep?" Maurice asked.

Before Francis could answer, a young woman with long hair dyed red and green arrived and leaned on the table waiting for them to order.

"Do you have croissants?" Maurice asked.

"No. We have biscuits." She responded as if the task of waiting tables fell far beneath her true talents. Maurice looked over his glasses at Francis as if asking for help.

"Give us two orders of pancakes and sausage, two coffees, and two small orange juices." Francis ordered for both of them. "I slept fine. I don't remember hitting the bed, but I remember the feeling that I was still in the airplane. I hate jet lag."

"If you drink orange juice, they say it helps." Maurice gave advice as if he had made a formal study of the issue. "We will be picked up at nine by an associate of the project."

"You have associates in America?" Francis swirled his coffee with a spoon as he asked his questions.

"If you will excuse me, Francis, may I ask why you seem to always stir everything before you drink?"

"Oh, it's an old habit. So, are your associates pleased with the samples we sent them from the Baltic?"

"I have not heard from them. The samples will take a few days to get there. What are your impressions of the Baltic compared to here?"

"The Baltic was a stinking sewer. At least the smell here isn't as rancid." Francis upturned his nose. "How many tons of raw sewage and untreated waste go into the Baltic per year?"

"It is inestimable at this point. Much less than it used to since the Soviets quit spending money on collective farms."

"The dead zone is massive. Do you think it extends as far as the surveys show, 100,000 kilometers?"

"I think perhaps farther. However, it is not only the width of the dead zone the Baltic has problems moving water throughout its depths as well. New deposits of fresh water cannot penetrate to the bottom. I expect a complete collapse of the ecosystem in the next decade unless something radical happens."

The waitress returned and dropped the plates onto the table. The silverware bounced as the plates landed. Maurice grimaced at the lack of service. The pancakes were small and burned on the outside rims. The sausage stood in a puddle of grease. Maurice pushed at the pancakes with his fork making the same upturned nose Francis had used to describe the Baltic. A small sprig of parsley lay on the side of the plate seeming oddly out of place.

"Maurice, I've been thinking about the stellar water."

"Yes?"

"How much is there?"

"Not much."

"Are we talking about liters or milliliters?"

"Perhaps a liter." Maurice seemed to be doing a calculation as he answered. "Maybe a little more."

"Can we have access to it?" Francis was excited.

"I can get a few milliliters of it, but the source is highly guarded and I have to go through several levels of approved request for the smallest sample, but yes, I can get some for our experiments. As you know a droplet is worth millions when you take into consideration what it took to get it back from space. More is coming."

"Are you certain?"

"But of course."

"The Cassini space probe? Is that how it will arrive?"

Maurice lowered his voice and leaned across the table toward Francis. "Not officially. The world would not understand that we are bringing extraterrestrial water back to the Earth. They would demand quarantine and sharing with all the other nations of the planet and you can imagine all the problems.

"I understand. My concern is the uncontrollable spontaneous effect that would occur if it were introduced to the ocean directly. What if by some freak accident it spilled into the sea as the probe reentered the atmosphere."

"Francis, the container is sealed. This is not a realistic worry, my friend. Besides, we have no way of knowing how many meteors have already deposited ancient water on the Earth or into the oceans. Perhaps as much as we have obtained naturally falls unobserved to the Earth on a regular basis."

"I still have a concern about the rapid biotic development we saw when the star water was added to the sea water. I am concerned that introducing a sample of this water into the sea may lead to a massive explosion of life forms and cause the oceans to lose the balance of life that has developed over millions of years."

"Francis, I cannot overstate the safety efforts we are using to contain the water. Introduction into the ocean is not going to happen unless it is planned under strict protocols. Now, can we leave this topic for a moment and finish eating so we can make our rendezvous?"

Francis knew from experience that the best plans may go astray. He finished his pancake and his second cup of coffee and followed Flauneau outside. An open air jeep was parked in front of their hotel with a smiling woman behind the wheel. Flauneau greeted her with obligatory cheek kisses. Francis extended his hand as he was introduced.

"Marquette, this is Professor Allenton."

"I am pleased to make your acquaintances." The woman stumbled with her English. She was deeply tanned and her dark hair was pulled back into a tight ponytail that emerged from under a Nike hat. "We will be pleasing to travel some quarter of an hour, perhaps not more than."

Flauneau piled the water collection kits in the back of the jeep. The tires squealed as Marquette pulled away from the curb. Several cars honked and barely missed her.

"Fools everywhere I go." Flauneau yelled. He pushed his fist into the air as an insulting gesture. "Can't anyone drive anymore?"

The dock soon came into view. Beyond it, the Gulf scene looked like a postcard. A few shrimp boats were putting out to sea followed by flocks of gulls. A large cabin cruiser waited there with motors running. As Francis followed the other two, he noticed an odd logo on the side of the boat, a painting of the sea with many hands thrust into it. The boat pulled out almost as soon as the trio stepped on its deck. Francis had not been out to sea for several years and enjoyed the feeling at the front of the boat as the sea spray formed an envelope of moisture around him. The boat reached trim in the water and the heavy motors hummed as the shore seemed to be pushed away from them.

After thirty or forty minutes had passed, the boat reduced thrust and slowed to a stop. Flauneau and Marquette made themselves busy opening the collection bags and putting labels on the bottles.

"It doesn't look dead." Francis observed.

"Oh, yes, she is very much the dead." Marquette responded pointing to the water all around them.

Flauneau and Marquette continued to talk and prepare the bottle. Occasionally they would both look at Francis then go back to their private conversation.

Marquette came over to Francis and handed him some sample bottles with lines attached. "You have made study of the ancient waters?"

"Yes, that's my work."

"I have been read of you."

"I see."

"You are suggesting that the water is healing?"

"Yes, in certain circumstances."

"I grew up in Lourdes."

"So, you know the stories of the miracles. Do you know anyone that was cured?"

"No. This all happened before me, I mean before I was born. Maurice says you have a wife."

"I'm a lucky man."

"Pardone?"

"It's just an expression. Yes. Her name is Cassidy."

"What a peculiar name for a woman. Is she being a scientist as well?"

"No, a nurse actually and a very good one."

"Are you married long?" she asked as she bent over in front of him, her top revealing cleavage.

"Just barely." Francis noticed Flauneau was smiling at him from across the deck.

"Come, Francis, help me put these out before you fall in." Flauneau laughed and held up the containers.

Just then Francis saw two sharks swimming near the boat. "Maurice, I thought we were in the dead zone."

"The sonar reading tells me we are in the dead zone. The sharks are among the last to leave. The other fish are dazed and easy prey, but before long the sharks will move out to sea. I want you to cast out the bottle and let it sink until the red mark on the line is right at the water's surface. At that point you must pull up the bottle quickly. I have a container for the sample."

The day was hot and the air very still. The men took off their tops to keep cool as they worked. Marquette did the same. She seemed to have no modesty whatsoever. Perhaps it was her European background, Francis thought. He turned after allowing himself a few indulgent looks and decided to focus on the work of gathering samples.

When they had collected their samples, the boat was turned to make her way back. Before they reached the dock, Maurice handed Marquette and Francis cold beers from a well-stocked refrigerator. Marquette had placed her top under her head as a makeshift pillow and was lounging in the sun. Her dark skin gleamed with sweat.

As Francis finished his first beer and reached for another. Marquette took a box from the cooler and a bag from beside her seat. She passed around the croissants along with cheese, grapes, and thin slices of meat. Then getting herself another beer, she moved over into some shade provided by an awning that cast a shadow on the deck. She fixed her eyes on Francis.

"Maurice tells me you have romantic in your ideas."

"Romantic?"

"Yes, that you believe in the Gaia Theory."

"It has some interesting ideas within it, but I would say I am more a pragmatic man and rely upon the scientific methods."

"So, it is more your wife that influences you?"

"She has a good mind." Francis had not defended his wife to another woman since he had married. He felt uncomfortable in the role. "Gaia Theory has some interesting interpretations of evolutionary activity."

"Tell me how you have come to your thinking on this." Marquette insisted.

"Life on Earth several million years ago began to react to the climate and other factors. This allowed changes in how bacteria and algae processed carbon dioxide and they produced oxygen as a by-product of living.

When they would produce too much oxygen, the Earth would produce a phyla or species that consumed it so a balance would be achieved. The cumulative action of millions of living things produced changes in the atmosphere. Viewed from one perspective the Earth appears to be very much alive and calculating how it can survive. The changes could be attributed to intelligence."

"Do you say the Earth has—I mean, do you agree with the Gaias that Earth knows what to do, it really can regulate itself by knowing?" Marquette had drawn her legs beneath herself and was sitting facing Francis.

"The super-organism theory implicit in the Gaia Theory suggests that the Earth knows when it is threatened and takes actions to save itself. The self-preserving instinct that is the hallmark of a living entity seems to have supportive evidence if you look at it from that perspective."

"And what is your perspective?"

"That life and the planet evolved in concert with each other. Neither has a remote awareness of the other. They maintain an almost perfect balance. Yet, man can upset the balance with pollution and other invasive activities."

"So, your wife is wrong?"

"No, not really — "

"How do you explain hysteresis then?" Flauneau interjected himself into the conversation.

Francis turned toward him, "I take it by hysteresis you mean the delayed impact of events upon the Earth to a point that it cannot correct itself?"

Flauneau was fully engaged, "Yes, a delayed, yet systemic reaction that becomes catastrophic. There was a point in the Earth's history that so much carbon dioxide existed that it should have driven off all of the available oxygen but that did not happen. Additionally, if hysteresis were operational then the Baltic would never have repaired itself. The Earth does seem to find a way to correct itself. The big jelly fish came and ate the little ones and all was set back into order. Explain that if you can, Doctor Allenton."

"I can't, at least I can't explain it by either approach. If the Earth is self-correcting then we would not see extinctions based on man's activities. If the Earth is not self-correcting then it would not produce the aberrations and adaptations needed to sustain life on Earth. What's your take on it, Marquette?"

Marquette turned to Maurice and responded rapidly in French.

Francis listened and then said, "Maurice, that was too fast for me. Please help me here."

"She says that she thinks the Earth is not a closed system but a part of a universal system larger than mankind can imagine. It is marching to a rhythm that we cannot see. The self-correcting and self-saving capacity may respond to activity in the far end of the universe, unknown and unseen, but not unfelt. She's Pagan, Francis, part of the sisterhood of old."

"She's talking Chaos Theory, the butterfly effect?" Francis tried to interpret her meaning as translated by Maurice.

"Well, yes and no. She's actually talking Gaia theory. Marquette and I have had a lot of discussions. She is talking Gaia on a scale we cannot imagine. Not only is the Earth self-correcting, but it holds a place in a solar system and a galaxy that also self-corrects. There is a process and interaction that is larger than the mind of man can see. It is like a little ant on the street corner sees only its block of sidewalk, yet just beyond the ant's view is a vastness unimaginable and unimagined."

"So, should we leave her alone, Marquette?" Francis asked. "Should we let Mother Earth tend to herself?"

Maurice listened again to Marquette's rapid French response and interpreted for Francis, "She says that our arrogance makes the things taking place now, such as pollution and extinction, to be important because it is taking place as we live on the Earth. We only want to save the Earth in order to save ourselves. If we were allowing ourselves to see a million years into the future, a small amount of time if you consider that we afford ourselves the luxury of looking backwards hundreds of millions of years at the fossil record, then we would see that our activity is meaningless in the machinery of time. That's how she sees it. We have no choice but to leave the Earth alone."

"So the environmentalists are wrong? Is that what you are saying, Marquette?" Francis pushed further, perhaps because he enjoyed a spirited conversation or perhaps because the beers had begun to make him bold.

Marquette spoke in English, "Not wrong in our time. But our time is but a moment in the celestial clock. We are so arrogant. We imagine that we can correct the machinery of the universe. The Earth Mother knows best what to do."

"Does it not also reflect our love?" Maurice interjected

"Love?" Marquette and Francis asked simultaneously.

"Yes. It reflects the love we have of our planet, our life and our comfort with how things run. We are creatures of this world. Do you think the algae or the butterfly love the world or their lives and places in it less than we do?"

Francis had come to like Maurice. He was a man of science but Maurice's heart began to emerge as the better part of his development. Francis did not have an answer.

The boat pulled close to the dock. Marquette put her top back on and taking a beer from the cooler, rubbed it across her forehead. The heat of the Gulf had arisen.

"Hot and sultry." Francis said as he jumped to the dock.

"Pardon." Maurice replied.

"The day's hot and sultry, isn't it?" Francis repeated but Maurice noticed he was looking at Marquette as he spoke.

All three were quiet as they climbed into the Jeep and returned to the hotel. Francis bid them good evening as he got down from the Jeep.

Marquette leaned toward Francis. "Do you have plans for supper?"

Francis looked at Flauneau who was staring at Marquette.

Francis turned back to her and responded, "No, but — "

She smiled, reached behind her, and handed him a sack, "Perhaps it would please you to eat the remaining croissant, fruit, and cheese."

Francis took the sack, thanked her, told Flauneau good evening and went to his room. He wondered if Flauneau had also thought Marquette was inviting him to eat supper with her. He stood by the struggling air conditioner and looked out the window at the Gulf while he ate his supper.

When he turned around, he saw the flashing message light on the telephone, but the decrepit hotel's voice mail worked poorly. He tried several times to get the message. He could tell it was Cassidy's voice. She sounded so far away. Francis looked at his clock. It was just after midnight in Paris. She might still be awake, but when he sat down on the edge of the bed extreme tiredness overtook him. He laid back and fell asleep in his clothes.

Chapter 12

The insistence of the ringing phone awakened Francis. He hoped it was Cassidy.

"Hello."

"Doctor Allenton, this is David Pearl. I'm a friend of Cassidy."

"What time is it?"

"Four-thirty."

"In the morning?"

"Of course. I wanted to take you out this morning. There is something I want you to see, and someone I want you to meet."

"Four-thirty?"

"Four-thirty-five now."

"I don't know, I mean, I suppose — David, when?"

"I'm outside the hotel now. Throw on some clothes. I've got some doughnuts and coffee. The boat has a galley on it."

"The boat?"

"Yes, come on will you."

"Fine. You know Cassidy?"

"Did know, back in college. She told me she had told you all about it."

"It?"

"Make it five minutes. I'll be outside in the old Volkswagen."

"Fine. I was only asleep."

"Huh?"

"Nothing, just a little morning humor."

Francis dressed and found his way downstairs and saw a vintage Volkswagen in front of the hotel. He approached the driver's window. It was rolled down a couple of inches. The man inside tried to stick his hand out through the opening. "Window won't roll down. Come around and let yourself in."

Francis walked around and opened the door to climb in. There was no place for his feet with the piles of trash, brochures and such on the floor. He stepped in noticing a brochure next to his foot that had a picture of a well-dressed business man holding a gun to the Earth. The caption said, "They're killing our Mother."

"What year is this bug?"

"Sixty-four."

"I thought the sixties."

"I'm saving up for a split window, maybe a fifty-five."

"I had a bug in college. These things always start, huh?"

"Not this one."

Francis noticed that the red warning lights on the dash glowed suggesting the engine was in peril.

"Thanks for getting up. Sorry about the early call. I like to get out on the water before the sun comes up."

"It's wet no matter when you get there." Francis said through a large protracted yawn.

David tossed him a bag of doughnuts and motioned to a cup of coffee in a cardboard holder.

When some the coffee had settled into the place that opened Francis' mind, he tried conversation again, "You met Cassidy in college?"

"Yeah. She was so — ah — smart. We were both in the Sierra Club. I turned her on to the whole Gaia thing. I took it pretty seriously but she was a 'newbie'."

"What's a newbie?"

"You know, all attitude and enthusiasm as long as it didn't get in the way of her going to classes. So we used to hang out, but I came south and didn't get around to finishing school. She's a nurse, right?"

"Yeah, darn good one."

They drank coffee and ate their doughnuts in silence for a few minutes while David drove through the empty streets to an old wharf.

"It's freaking beautiful this morning." David said spitting small doughnut fragments as he spoke. The bug stopped with brakes that squealed. David turned it off and left the keys in the ignition. "Trust me, nobody would want it." He got out and reaching behind the driver's seat retrieved a small bag. "Come on. Let's get on board before she sinks.

Francis followed David down the dock and stepped over the edge of the old boat. "Francis, cast off that bow line, will you?" David started the motors and headed into the Gulf. The old boat responded well to the waves. Francis thought it reminded him of a pirate ship, rough on the outside but strong where it counts. The seats were wet from the morning dew and there were few places to sit that had not been piled with equipment of some sort.

David spoke loudly above the motor noise, "I was into the Eco-Extremism and Cass didn't want to drop out of school or go to jail, so we just kept in touch. I was with the first reef check."

"Reefer?"

"No, I'm not a dope head if that's what you're thinking. I worked for Save Our Seas in Hawaii at the National Center for Coastal Ocean Science in 1999. Didn't you write an article for the Nitrogen Transport and Transformation for S.C.O.P.E.?"

"Yes, that was me. It seems a long time ago now. I was concerned about pollution in the Gulf area." Francis had moved to the cabin and stood next to David as he pushed some charts around and steered the wheel with his knee.

"That's why we are talking."

"Why?"

"I want you to see the Gulf. They are building something weird out there, and I can't get a grip on what it is. I think you might know what it is."

"What kind of weird?"

"I don't know, weird. Like on the Twilight Zone." He sang the "do dee, do dee" mimicking the theme song. "I can't get close, but I thought you might be able to understand what they were doing. There are containers that look like heavy water containers from Canada."

"Heavy water?"

"Yeah. Did you see that shit in the paper? Some kids died. Eco-terrorism is my guess or a secret government experiment gone wrong. I went on a protest up there a few years ago. They are spewing that shit all over Lake Huron. We broke into the facility where they kept the heavy water. They sell it all over the world."

"Are you sure it's heavy water?"

"I will never forget those barrels of heavy water, the markings on them and the week I spent in a Canadian jail. These kinds of things stay with you. I also saw some barrels marked ESA. What the hell is ESA?"

"European Space Agency?"

"Is that what ESA stands for?"

"Well, that's what it stands for in Europe."

"Damn, what are those rapists doing to Her now?"

It seemed to Francis that David spoke of Mother Earth as if she were his actual mother. He obviously embraced the ideas of radical environmentalism.

"You know something about heavy water, don't you?" David asked.

"I do. Technically it is called tritium and is a mutagenic."

"So, mutations."

"Yes, when you introduce heavy water to a bio-diverse area the results almost always cause mutations of the natural species during embryonic formation."

"Five-eyed frogs, that kind of thing?" David asked. He looked at the chart again and made a course correction.

"Yes, but the most damage is to pregnant women — the development of the embryo. Oh, by the way, Cassidy is pregnant."

"Oh?" The news of Cassidy's pregnancy didn't seem to register with David. "We were in Canada to protest tritium emissions. They were screwing up the food chain in Lake Huron. Do you think they are dumping the tritium here in the Gulf? I mean, do you think they are doing toxic dumping here?"

"I wouldn't see why. They can dump it with impunity in their own lake."

"How pregnant?" David asked as if the comment about Cassidy had just registered.

"Just."

"Congratulations. You know, if you scientists would get your shit together, children would inherit a much cleaner world than the one you are now handing them."

"Not every scientist is working to pollute the Earth. Some of us are working to clean it up."

"How so?" David began to reduce the engine throttle.

"I'm looking into altering the dead zones by introducing a species that feeds on the phytoplankton."

"You're not serious?"

"I am."

"How do you know what the new species will do over time?"

"Well, it's just a theory so far."

"No, I mean it, man. I'm serious. You don't want to be putting anything into the soup that Mother Nature hasn't already put there."

"It's not a new species, well, not exactly. It's a mutation of an existing species, one that is predatory on the plankton."

"Man, we need the plankton. It produces most of the oxygen on Earth. Don't go messing with that shit."

"Plankton is the main cause of the dead zones."

"Bullshit, man, it's pollution that is causing the dead zones. Industrialized waste pours into the Gulf and the water is dead all the way down the water column."

"Well, that's not exactly how it works. The plankton blooms because they feed on the nitrates. The blooms prevent the lower levels from having sunlight penetrate and the whole thing starts a process that results in the dead zone."

"Yeah, like I said, it's the stinking industrialists that are doing it, aided, I might add, by scientists."

"Well, farmers are responsible as much as factories."

"No way, man! You got your facts on backwards. It's the Man that pushes the little farmer out of the way and they use whatever they want to grow their cash crops and they don't care what it kills as long as they make money. Fuckers!"

"People have become accustomed to having food." Francis offered, but he could tell his argument was wasted. David had already decided to blame industrialization for the problems in the Gulf. Perhaps, in some ways, he was right.

"You just leave her alone. Mother will fix it. She will fix it all. Come the day Mother Nature will rise up and extinguish man the way she did the dinosaurs. She's got a plan. It may take a million years, but she's going to win. I'd just like to be around to see her start kicking their asses."

"Are you against regulating pollution?"

"No way. I'm on board with that. Let's shut the suckers down." David was getting on a roll, his voice becoming nearly a rhythmic rap. He bobbed his head as he spoke to some unheard but obviously felt beat.

"If you shut them down, aren't you taking Mother's place? It seems to me you either have to let Her go or help Her."

"How do you know what help is, man? Biologists introduced species to clean up one problem only to find that they created a larger problem. You don't know enough to help. We can try to keep the Man off her back by controlling pollution, but even then we aren't really the deciding force. Ultimately, Mother knows best."

The boat slowed about two hundred yards from a platform floating in the Gulf. The site seemed shut down. Nothing seemed to be happening. A single large white boat was tied to the gangway. It was the same boat Francis had been on yesterday. The logo was obvious.

"I know that boat." Francis told David.

"How?"

"I was on it all day yesterday."

"Who owns it?"

"I don't know. It was waiting for us. I thought it was a charter."

"Man, you're an idiot. People don't charter a high dollar boat like that. There is some money behind those props. What's that logo mean?"

"I told you, David, I don't know."

"I'm going in to get a closer look."

"I'm not sure that's such a good idea."

"You can't be timid and be an environmentalist, Francis. You have to walk right into the lion's mouth and pull out his fangs."

"That's a good philosophy if you want to be the first thing eaten for supper. Let's circle around a little closer. Hand me those binoculars." Francis held out his hands.

David gunned the motor on the boat and they began to approach the platform. David continued to move closer to the platform than Francis felt reasonable. He looked nervously from his binoculars to David several times. David swung around and maintained about a hundred yard distance from the platform where two men emerged in light-colored jump suits. The larger of the two men lifted binoculars and Francis could see the other one writing something, probably the identification numbers on David's boat.

"That's enough, David."

"Can you see anything?"

"I don't see containers or anything on the decks."

"They were all there yesterday."

"Well, there aren't any there now."

Francis looked through the binoculars again. He thought one of the men was using a cell phone. "I bet they wrote down your boat numbers and he's calling someone."

"This is a well-known boat in the area. I've been all over the Gulf causing these rapists grief. I've been arrested a dozen times for trespass, but that's what I do. I'm a barnacle on the butt of polluters."

"Well, that's enough. I have to get back. We are flying back to Europe tomorrow."

"I think I could get a little closer." David seemed to be taunting Francis.

"Perhaps another day, okay?" Francis said in a stern voice.

"Oh, man, the fun was just starting."

David swung the boat away and headed back to the old wharf. They didn't talk much on the way back. Francis was determined not to come across to David as weak or lacking a spirit of adventure, but he was a family man now and he couldn't see any reason to take unnecessary risks.

David dropped him off at the hotel. The Volkswagen died in the parking lot and David crawled beneath the rear of the car and banged on the starter with a wrench. It protested as he got back in and tried to start it.

"She's a piece of shit," he yelled to Francis, "but I still love her." When the car started, he sped away. A large plume of burned oil smoke arose into the air behind the bug.

Flauneau came out to the parking lot.

"Who's that?"

"An old friend of the family."

"He looks like a hippie."

"He's all right. He's an environmentalist."

Both men waved the fumes away from their faces. Francis chuckled at the irony of the moment, the car was doing damage to the same environment that David was trying to repair.

Chapter 13

The flight back to Paris seemed endless. After two stopovers, they finally touched down. Flauneau and Francis shared a taxi. When they pulled in front of the apartment, Francis could see the curtains move as Cassidy peeked out. He was anxious to see her.

"We begin in earnest tomorrow." Maurice said.

"Yes. I am particularly interested in seeing the samples of the ancient water."

"Would you say you are also an environmentalist, Francis?"

"Why do you ask?"

"I'm not entirely certain our goals are compatible."

"We are both interested in saving the oceans."

"Yes, but we are attempting to bring about change by introducing the effects of the stellar water. Many environmentalists demand we leave everything alone, just as it is, and trust that Mother Nature will fix herself."

"I'm confident that if the dead zones can be healed, environmentalists will be the first to give support."

"Don't be so certain of that. There is a division between science and environmental preservationists. They think we are the devils. They call us rapists."

Francis found it interesting to hear Maurice use the exact terms David had used.

"Maurice, I've heard this before, but they live in an idealized world of what they think will happen if we just leave things alone. They talk out of both sides of their mouths at the same time. They want to reduce pollution and at the same time they want to leave everything alone. It's hard to have it both ways. Either you trust the planet can heal itself or you trust that Mother Nature needs a hand."

Maurice reached over and laid his hand on Francis' arm. "I'm just saying that the funding agencies of this project are very much inclined to bring about a change in the dead zones by introducing a technology that they can own and sell. It's not unlike the people that sell the membranes that are used to soak up the oil spills in the ocean. The environmentalists would say that we have no right to plunder the earth and take the oil and move it by sea to be consumed. Pragmatic people see that oil is going to be taken and sometimes, even if every precaution is taken, it may spill and if it does spill a technology needs to be ready to clean it up the best we can. Sometimes commerce and environmentalism do not make good bedfellows."

At that moment Cassidy came out onto the front stoop. She waved at Francis.

Francis was grateful for the rescue. "We'll talk more of this later, Maurice. Thanks for driving me home. Say hello to your wife for me when you get home."

"I have no wife. I have a partner."

"Well, all the same, say hello to her for me."

"I will say hello to him when I get home."

"Oh, I'm sorry, I was unaware — "

Maurice said nothing as Francis fell over his own efforts to remain neutral about Maurice's revelation. Francis remembered all their conversations, a dozen touches to his arm that he had interpreted as innocent, not provocative. He stood outside the car trying to think of something to say.

"Until tomorrow then." Maurice said. He put the car into gear and sped away without looking at Francis.

Francis bounded up the steps taking them two at a time. Cassidy's arms were open. They embraced and he started lifting her off the ground as was his habit but stopped and put her down. "Sorry. How's the momma?"

"Fine, how's the daddy?"

"I'm good. I'm tired, of course. You remember the flight when we came over. It seems to last forever."

"Did you get my message about David?"

"No. Your message was all messed up. We were staying in a pitiful old hotel on the Gulf. Their voice mail system must have sand in it. My God, you should have seen the pool, it was awful. So much hurricane damage, so little recovery."

"Poor baby, jet setting around the world and you want sympathy from me."

"It really was horrible. But, I met him. We went out on the Gulf."

"What?"

"Yes, I went out with David to see a Gulf platform. He is a little, ah, extreme, shall I say."

"Well, duh! That's what I told you on the message. He is an extremist and will do just about anything for a thrill. I called to warn you not to go anywhere with him, just talk to him."

"Great, now I find out. He was driving an old bug."

"Not *the* bug? Probably the same car he had in college. How long is his hair now?"

"It's cut short — well longer than mine, but, maybe because it's thinning."

"No! David with thinning hair? It was so long in college it was past his waist. Is he still chasing the Big Man?"

"Yes, the great evil ones with whom all scientists are complicit in a plot to destroy the Earth for financial gains, or so he says."

"He's a little on the deep side with some of his ideas, but basically he is probably right. Greed will stop at nothing to make short term money, even if it destroys the Earth. Greed doesn't care what kind of world is left behind. David left school to go on the first reef watch."

"He mentioned that. He said it was in the eighties."

"Yeah, eighty-two I think. He never came back to school."

"So, were you guys serious or anything?"

"I was a freshman and he was fun, that's all. Why? What did he say?" Cassidy opened her eyes wide as if expecting a revelation of some past indiscretion.

Francis watched her and offered, "Oh, not much. He mentioned a couple of orgies and such."

"Oh, sure. Shut up! He did not. Besides, he was always high so I doubt he remembers anything of those days."

"So, you're not denying the orgies."

Cassidy gave him an exasperated look. She adroitly changed the topic, "What did you find in the Baltic and the Gulf? Are they dead?"

"We took water samples at several locations and depths and we're going to take a look at the samples tomorrow. We saw a bunch of sharks out in the Gulf, but they will leave soon, they say, since they won't have any thing to prey on. Flauneau says the funding behind the project wants to repair the oceans. David went ballistic when I told him that we were looking into altering the plankton or introducing a predatory species to control the dead zones."

"I can't blame him for that. I've been doing a lot of thinking about this project idea and I want to talk. Are you too tired? I haven't talked to anyone except the doctor and the woman at the market."

"I'm not too tired. What's up?" Francis held her close to his side as they moved to sit on the divan.

"It's the Gaia Theory. I've had a troubling thought. What if nature is attempting to rid itself of the problems mankind is causing and by intervening you upset the balance."

"Tell me more." Francis reached over and slid his suitcase closer to he could put his feet up on it. He undid the first button on his shirt knowing this would be a long conversation. Although he was tired, he admired Cassidy's thought processes and valued the chance to interact with her, especially when he was puzzling over the same subject.

"Well, my thoughts go along like this. People are organisms upon which other organisms live. Mites and other things such as bacteria all thrive on our skins and inside our guts. The mites on our skin go about their business unaware of the consciousness of their hosts. They cannot imagine that the place where they live is part of a larger organism that has ideas, hopes, and dreams. As long as they can eat and reproduce they are content to live in that ignorance. They exploit their host in the same manner humans exploit the Earth.

"The self-regulating capacity of the host organism keeps things pretty much in check. We can't have too many of one kind of parasite or life form living on us or within us. In some ways we need them to help digest food and clean us up, so we have formed an intimate relationship with them. We are, for the most part, unaware of them and they are unaware of us, until a breach of balance occurs. Then we take action to rid ourselves of them. If our gut gets churned up with too many flu bacteria we take action to control them or reduce their numbers to the point of reaching balance again."

Cassidy paused and Francis responded, "Yes, I agree. We are all infested on a daily basis and for the most part, we are unaware of them and they are unaware of us."

"So, Francis, the Earth as a living organism does the same thing. The shifts in nature may all be similar to the self-regulating activity within the human body. I'm even more aware of these ideas as I feel Baby Francis growing in me. So, what if Earth is attempting to snuff out mankind the way we would try to eliminate flu bugs? If they threaten our health, we take no more notice of killing a colony of bacteria than the Earth might take of eliminating the human species by the millions in order to save Herself. We have polluted the Earth, made Her sick, and upset Her natural balances. She will act to protect Herself. The fight against our extinction is futile if the Earth has decided that mankind is an irritant and must go."

While she spoke, Francis made his glasses move up and down on his forehead using his face muscles, his long-time habit while listening.

When she paused again, he encouraged her. "Go on."

"I'm just saying if a process is in place in which the Earth has determined that mankind is a threat then attempting to correct things might cause further shifts, actions leading to reactions and actions to counteract those actions leading to further actions until a crisis is upon us. Perhaps it is better to leave things alone."

"And let the Earth snuff us out?" Francis asked.

"Mankind is so arrogant. We think we can kill the Earth so we think we can fix it. Perhaps all of this is larger than we can see and ultimately, if the hands of time are left alone, perhaps we are not meant to dominate the Earth. Perhaps global warming and disease are the ways Earth is defending Herself. Perhaps She would set things back in order if there were a drastic reduction in oxygen breathing life forms. Perhaps it is the long term goal of the Earth to have only species living on the planet that fit a plan to preserve the balance that has sustained the Earth for millions of years. The predatory nature of the dinosaurs threatened the balance on Earth and now they are gone. Who can say that this isn't human destiny?"

Francis listened intently to Cassidy. He had learned to trust her global views and intuitions. When they first met, it was her sense of how things really were that had alerted him to the Water Cartel's true purposes. She was the one who had helped him puzzle through Alford Purlough's real intentions and the Water Cartel's plans to alter the mineral content of water provided to the military and national leaders. Francis was the one who had rushed headlong into the research process trusting it was about altering water to prevent injury and infection only to find he had been duped by his own enthusiasm. Cassidy rarely talked without purpose or postulated ideas on a whim. He knew it best to trust her, even when she was just putting ideas together. Those ideas most often would lead to an important conclusion.

"Science is intervention," he finally said. "It's what I do. I find a problem and research a solution, not for the sake of pure investigation, but because I want to have an answer."

"Can you know the long term consequences of your solution? If the Earth is making adjustments to your interventions, then what may seem to be an answer at one point in time may become a problem in the future."

"Well, Cassidy, if I look at it from your perspective, the Earth is struggling to find a solution to correct destructive human behaviors. Perhaps she needs a little help. I recall when we first met you were struggling with your own survival. You were about to undergo medical interventions for the cancer that had polluted your body. Healing waters from an Arkansas spring spiraled through the Caduceus brought health back to you. If we can find a way to heal the Earth's oceans, then don't we owe it to the Earth to set right the errors of what others have done?"

"Yes, I see your point. Do you know where there are a lot of frogs?"

"Excuse me?"

"Mount Saint Helens."

"And this has to do with?" Francis knew it was going somewhere.

"My point, Francis. When Mount Saint Helens erupted, it laid waste miles of forests and creatures in its pathway. You would expect it all to be a wasteland, but as we speak, life is returning in abundance and in unexpected ways to the area. Let me explain. The frogs were hibernating when the volcano erupted, thus they were spared. However, the trees that shaded the ponds where they lived and bred were knocked down and algae grew in abundance because the water had direct sunlight. Therefore, tadpoles thrived in the environment, and the frog population exploded. Now creatures that feed on frogs will thrive, and those that feed on the predators of the frogs will thrive, and eventually a balance, a revitalization will result. Earth set right the consequences of that eruption. Do you think She lacks the ability to do less on a global level?"

"I don't know — "

Cassidy interrupted, "I think we will eventually pollute the Earth, the water, the air, and the land so much that it will result in the loss of life."

"And then?" Francis asked.

"Well, and then, some of the people of the Earth will die either from starvation, or war over scarce resources, or from epidemics."

"And then?" Francis asked.

"More people will die."

"So, eventually there will be fewer people on Earth or perhaps all the people on Earth will perish."

"Right."

"And then?"

"And then there won't be any people, and therefore, there won't be any further pollution or denigration of the seas, the water, the air, and the land. You see, the dead zones in the ocean will result in the loss of sea life that man has used as a food source. If the food sources vanish, the populations that depend upon them will die, and Mother Earth will prevail. The irritant will be gone and the land will return to balance. Earth will have regulated Herself successfully."

Francis let the strength of her argument sink in. It seemed a flawless argument if the Earth was a living and conscious entity. It would act out of self-preservation and eliminate the life form that threatened her existence.

"But this whole argument presumes that the Earth is a living and thinking organism. We don't know this."

"Neither do the hair mites that live on our skin or the bacteria that live in our guts, but nonetheless, we are still live and thinking creatures even if they are not aware of our consciousness."

"So, you propose we stand by and let the Earth flick us off into the void?"

"We have no choice." Cassidy looked at him, "Francis, do you think the dinosaurs had a choice? I'm sure they fought to stay alive and did what they could to manipulate their environment, but the process is a super process, beyond their capacity to make a difference. What living thing can imagine its own extinction?"

Her logic was flawless. Yet the scientist in Francis rebelled against the notion of neutrality or lack of action in the face of a coming crisis. He looked into the eyes of this person he loved and could not imagine a world without her. While not a religious person, at least not a part of organized religion, he had always believed that man was created in the likeness of God. The notion that God would stand idly by while mankind plummeted into extinction seemed wrong. He leaned even closer to her and spoke softly, "And what of the future generations, our own baby for instance?"

"I know. It bothers me, too, but being pregnant really made me think about all of this. These processes may take millions of years and can't be seen or felt in a single lifetime. The effects of pollution, the loss of clean water, all of these things can be felt, but the cosmic consequences are so large and so distant that we cannot know the things to do."

"But, Cassidy, you are an environmentalist. You have struggled to save the Earth however and wherever you can."

"Yes, but I must admit a certain kind of human centric arrogance within my beliefs. I have believed that I can make a difference on a world level. Yet there are times I find it hard to make a difference in my own life. Now I have a blessing and a responsibility as a parent. I have a responsibility to that new life and a responsibility to the Earth that will sustain that life. They are not mutually exclusive responsibilities, rather they are inclusive. One is bound to the other. In a selfish way I want my child and my life to be sustained and be comfortable, safe, and happy. But should I want less for the very planet that gives it all to me?"

"We must do what we can."

"And if the doing is against the will of the Earth? Do we presume we know what to do and how to do what must be done?"

"We know from science that the effects of pollution can be reversed."

"Do we? Data will show us what happened in the span of a single life or perhaps a generation or two, but the level of which I am speaking is a hundred million generations. Should we trust in that process or trust in ourselves?"

"We can't just stand by and let the Earth collapse around us."

"We may be powerless to stop it. The weather patterns, the global warming, the loss of the Earth's vitality to produce food for the expanding populations, all these may be ways the Earth is preparing to rid herself of mankind's toxic infection."

"Well, that's all very good and well if you are a microbe, but we are people."

"People may be only microbes to the universe."

"I can't stand by and watch it all go to hell."

"Nor can you really prevent it."

"I will have to try, for you, for me, for little Francis, for the world in general, we must try."

"Yes, Francis, I suppose you must. The research I've been doing has formed in my mind as a collective gestalt. I think I have seen a large and complex picture, too large and complex to comprehend. I have a strong feeling about it. It is a change on a planetary level. I'm sure of it. Gaia is arising."

Chapter 14

Cassidy had initiated lovemaking which did help Francis overcome his worries about sex with his pregnant wife, but after that time of reassurance and relief, Francis still slept poorly. He found the ideas that Cassidy and he had discussed to be unsettling. He didn't want to believe that the efforts of science were wasted. He liked pushing and moving the world with ideas. He had dedicated his life to the prospects of positive change. Rather than be defeated by futility, he believed that one should redouble his efforts. Nothing, it seemed to Francis, was worse than defeat, unless it was apathy.

He could not reconcile how an environmentalist would choose apathy when faced with the certain destruction of the Earth from pollution and overuse of natural resources. He could not find a place inside himself to believe that the Earth would rise up and fix Herself. It was particularly difficult since he was the one that had brought about Cassidy's healing from cancer. He had intervened and the recipient of his intervention lay beside him nurturing their unborn child.

As a scientist he doubted that a fountain of youth or a healing spring could exist, but as a person, even before having to face the death of one he loved, he wanted to believe in healing. Considering all of this, the idea that the Earth could heal others then opened the door that it could also heal itself. Perhaps all the changes that Cassidy mentioned taking place on Earth were efforts to rid the planet of the troublesome creatures it had spawned. These ideas plagued him, yet the next day he still arose, had his coffee, hugged Cassidy while patting her stomach, and went to the lab believing that persistence may guide wrong intentions and futile activities as much as it may guide brilliance.

Maurice was waiting with a broad smile on his face.

"What are you grinning at?" Francis asked.

"Just waiting for the honeymooner to arrive."

"Fantasies of newlywed antics are much exaggerated I fear. Did you stay up all night with your partner?"

"Oh, yes, it was a night to remember. I think I fell asleep on the divan as Rene played Solitaire. Are you ready to begin?"

"We have strict containment, don't we?" Francis asked. "I don't want to be part of something that would accidentally spread a foreign species through the Earth's oceans."

Francis looked at Maurice's preparations. The specimens were contained in sealed examination modules. The samples of dead zone water were clearly labeled.

Maurice explained, "Microscopic examination has revealed a large number of algae and other plankton in the samples. I have introduced a small amount of the ancient water into the specimen from the Baltic Sea dead zone area. The temperature inside the examination module has been raised to a point that promotes plankton growth. The specimens have been agitated slowly to insure complete mixing of the ancient water and the specimens. I have repeated the process with the specimen from the Gulf of Mexico dead zone in a separate module. Every precaution has been taken."

As Francis watched, Maurice removed a sample of the mixed water for examination under the microscope. The work was excruciatingly slow as the samples and the slides were prepared using robotic arms and grabbers behind thick glass. When the prepared slide was extracted and placed on the microscope viewing area, Francis watched as Maurice sat at the lab table, removed his glasses, and adjusted the lenses of the microscope.

"What's happening?" Francis asked.

"Nothing just now. The plankton are behaving normally. Perhaps a slight agitation. I wouldn't expect anything rapid. We will observe them every ten minutes for the next eight hours. If anything is going to happen, I believe it will happen in that time frame."

"Are you familiar with the term 'radical reaction mechanism,' Maurice?"

"Of course, Francis, I am aware of the inherent ability of micro-organisms to store compounds so if they are introduced to a hostile or toxic environment they can feed internally to survive. It is similar to how humans store fat for the possibility of a famine. In fact, some microorganisms have learned to use the toxic substances as food by breaking them down into carbons and feeding on them. There is some hope that this approach might work with toxic spills in the ocean."

"Yes, however, I am more interested in your opinion of the novel environmental conditions producing spontaneous mutations. In some studies the microbial life developed a surprising array of mutations in the toxic environment."

"Yes. I know of these studies. It seems that the mutations are spins-offs of the basic life form searching for a mutation that will let the species survive. Mutation married to Darwinian selection produces a survivor. The survivor is successful and breeds to produce a line of survivors and thus the basic organism is altered."

"Adaptive radiation results."

"Radiation?" Maurice asked.

"Not in the sense of isotopes. This is the radiation of the species from a single point of adaptation into the rest of the environment. Like how the limbs of a tree radiate outward."

"I see, radiating, rapid deployment of the mutation expands across the entire environment."

"Yes, and the most successful adaptation replaces the old form."

"You are concerned that the phytoplankton will make adaptations, perhaps even mutations?"

"Yes."

"If these mutations are successful and desired, they are called adaptations. If they are troublesome, we will call them mutations. If they develop into a predatory form that eats the planktons, it may be possible to reverse the dead zones."

Francis thought for a moment. He felt a growing obligation to place a caution in front of their results. "If they continue to adapt and mutate, perhaps making the leap from phytoplankton to zooplankton, then what? We will soon move from an adaptation to a mutation. When one part of the environment mutates, the rest of the environment mutates in response to it. We might unleash a Cambrian-like explosion of new life forms and mutations that cannot be controlled."

"Then the sea will change."

"Maurice, it is not our place to change the sea or introduce a new species to the Earth."

"Who can say?" Maurice protested. "It would not be a new species, just an adaptation of an already existing species. Man has introduced lots of mutations to serve his needs. Hunting dogs from wolves, for example."

"If it is beneficial in the short run, we will call it an adaptation, but if it runs wild and we lose control, it will be called a mutation. We will have produced an era of anthropogenics that may be beyond our control."

"Anthropogenics is already upon us, Francis. From the time man first plowed the Earth, fished the sea, or burned a forest to gain better planting, his mark has been upon the Earth."

"Yes, we have made our little mark upon the Earth, but this level of change is planetary-wide, it's — ."

"Can we wait to see the results of the stellar water on the samples before we declare the sky is falling?"

"I'm just cautious." Francis looked at Maurice.

"And I am not?" Maurice backed up as if insulted.

"That's not my suggestion. I just — "

"If we find rapid mutation of new life forms, then we will destroy the samples. That's all we can do. We need to see what happens."

"Are you confident about the containment system?"

"Yes. State of the art, space age and absolutely secure. It's time for the next observation."

Francis sat down in front of the microscope. A new sample of the combined dead zone water and stellar water had been placed on the slide. He took off his wire rim glasses and rubbed his eyes. Before him the phytoplankton seemed to be altering. He tried not to blink. One of them seemed to be moving. Perhaps it was his imagination but the phytoplankton, basically a primitive plant, seemed to be exhibiting locomotion. The ability to move through space is an aspect of a zooplankton, a life form.

"Maurice, do you know anything about radiolaria?" Francis asked.

"Plankton, I think. They just kind of floated around in the ocean currents, didn't they?"

"Yes. Some fossil records find their unusual spheroid shapes in the Cambrian period. I made a fairly exhaustive study of them during my initial investigation of the healing effects of spiraling water because they were shaped in a spiral form. They existed somewhere between animal and plant."

"Neither animal or plant?"

"Well, both actually. They could move around, reproduce sexually like animals or asexually like plants. They could either be opportunistic passive feeders or predatory. They seemed capable of rapid adaptation or mutation as situations presented themselves. They could develop flagella, for instance, if they were in a liquid setting. They could return to an amoeba state if they were in a solid structure. They have not been classified very well by micropaleontologists."

"Were they basically plankton that could move on their own in certain situations?"

"Yes, they were plankton but showing remarkable adaptability to situational demands to alter themselves."

"Why do you ask?" Maurice slid his stool close to Francis.

"Because I'm looking at some of them." Francis scooted his chair away from the microscope. "Look at the micron level."

Maurice rubbed his eyes and pushed himself against the eye pieces. He pushed back from the microscope and rubbed his eyes again. He picked up a piece of lens cleaning paper and rubbed the surfaces of the eye pieces. He looked again. "They have flagella."

"Yes. I saw them. Do you notice anything else?"

"They seem to be predatory in nature, killing the other plankton."

"Where in hell did they come from? Did you see any radiolaria in the sample water before the ancient water was added?"

"None." Maurice answered.

"You realize they didn't show up in the fossil record until the Cambrian explosion?" Francis felt agitated and excited at the same time.

"You're getting ahead of yourself, Francis. This doesn't prove anything."

"Let's look at the other sample."

Both men hurried to the other isolation chamber and waited impatiently as the slide was prepared. The robotic arm placed the slide on the viewing piece. Maurice was the first to look.

"Here they are again, Francis, only these are even more developed. The ancient water must have initiated their development. They are plankton-like creatures, but not plantlike at all in this state. They have come to life where none previously existed. Perhaps they lie dormant in the genetic structure?"

"Let's get some pictures. No one will believe this."

"This is the stuff of the Nobel Prize, Francis!"

"Perhaps."

"Not perhaps. This is astonishing."

"We need to keep them under observation."

"Of course. I'll take the first shift. It's late. Can you come tomorrow in the early morning? I will take pictures and keep notes on their development."

"I'll take the first shift. Really, I don't mind." Francis made a sincere offer.

"No. I insist. You have a pregnant wife at home. Rene will understand."

"The containment is more important now. You do understand this, Maurice."

"I understand."

"We must be certain."

"We have a lab protocol in place. It's the same that we used when we obtained the water samples from space. I stake my reputation on it."

"I'll be back in the morning then. Just one more look."

Francis bent over the eyepieces not bothering to sit. He let out a long sigh and shook his head from side to side.

"We may be looking at another Cambrian explosion in the making."

"I know." Maurice said. He had flipped open his laptop and was writing his observations.

Francis had been gone for less then twenty minutes when the phone rang. A technician summoned Maurice to the telephone.

"Maurice Flauneau." he answered.

"Monsieur Flauneau, this is Estan Milan."

"Yes?"

"We have been following your progress on our research project. Our colleague in the United States, Mister Halter, has expressed interest in your findings. As you know, we have been funding your research under the auspices of the G8. We are keenly interested in the results of the study."

"The results are inconclusive at the moment."

"We have had some information that you have allowed an American to join the team yet we do not recall any consultation with us concerning his involvement."

"I was under the impression I had a free hand on this project."

"Yes, to a certain extent. However, we have concerns about this man. He has a dubious reputation in America."

"Francis Allenton is a brilliant scientist. He has helped me immeasurably."

"Still, our partners are concerned about his involvement — concerned to such an extent that it might jeopardize the funding. Do I make myself clear?"

"I can assure you he is more concerned with security than I."

"Security is not the concern of which I am speaking."

"He has the most profound knowledge of ancient waters in the world."

"We had anticipated the use of a man from China on this project but he met with an untimely death."

"I can assure you that Francis, I mean Doctor Allenton, is not a threat to this project. He is making important contributions to our findings."

"What findings are these?"

"I meant to say that he would make the possibility of our findings more likely."

"Your admiration of Doctor Allenton may be clouding your senses, Maurice. We are aware that you hold certain men, in what shall I say, extreme admiration."

"This has nothing to do with my feelings for him. I admire the man for his talent."

"We are not certain that this partnership is in the best interest of the project."

"It's too late. He is already intimately involved. I need his perspective as we interpret our observations."

"Nevertheless, our American partners have expressed concern. Needless to say, they wish their concerns to remain confidential. Mister Halter is in France and will be arriving in Paris some time tomorrow. I expect this situation to be resolved before he arrives."

"Meaning what?"

"Resolved. Dr. Allenton must be gone."

Chapter 15

Francis unlocked the door and stepped inside the apartment. It had the smell of roses and strong cleaning fluid mixed together.

"What the hell is that smell?" he asked as he put down his briefcase.

"Don't ask." Cassidy turned the corner. She seemed pale. "Little Francis is making me puke my guts out. How was your day?"

"Not bad, discovered a new life form, that kind of thing."

"Go on! Really?" Cassidy wasn't always sure when Francis was serious with her.

"Yeah, well, at least I think so. We added some of the stellar water to the Gulf and Baltic Sea dead zone water and a new form of plankton emerged."

"Plankton is a plant, right?"

"Well, plankton is actually either a type of plant or a type of animal, both found in the ocean. The distinction is that phytoplankton, the plants, work by photosynthesis, and zooplankton, the little tiny animals, move about feeding on other living things. The ones I saw today I had only seen as fossils. They are a type of zooplankton that forms little crystalline shells in the shape of spirals."

"Here we go again."

"What?"

"It's just you and those spirals."

"Radiolaria."

"Radio who?"

"It's what we found today, radiolaria. None were present in the dead zone samples and now they are all over the place and they are predatory to the algae."

"Is that a good thing? I mean, is it good that they have appeared? I'm not certain the sudden appearance of an algae-eating life form is good news. Is it?"

"Well, they have been on Earth before. They developed rapidly in the Cambrian period, when life on Earth exploded."

"So, the plan is to have these little guys eat the other guys?"

"Not my plan. I'm just trying to determine how they showed up in the first place."

"But that is the plan, right?"

"I don't think we are anywhere near a plan. I'm just seeing what happens to the dead zone water when stellar water is introduced."

"Science for science sake?"

"That's my take on it."

"Don't think for a minute that if they eat the algae and clean up the dead zones that they won't be bottled and sold!"

"I have no information concerning how the findings are going to be used."

"I love you, dear Francis, but you have to wake up about how the world is currently working. It pollutes the planet and then seeks a technology to clean it up and then sells the technology to the world anxious about the future. It's what makes the world go around. Turn it to crap then invent a crap-eating enzyme and sell it to the highest bidder."

"I'm aware of how the world works, Sweetheart." Francis replied.

"You can't allow them to put anything into the water, not now and not ever."

"What are you worried about? If it cleans up the dead zones, the world will be a better place than it was before."

"You don't know what kind of water you are dealing with, from place to place or from day to day. Water in one part of the ocean is not the same as the water in another place."

"Of course not. The salinity varies."

"No, I'm talking about the seventy or eighty thousand chemicals in use across the world. We invent approximately another thousand every year. We study and understand in a very limited way what the effect of a single chemical has on life or the ecosystem. We don't know about the long term effect of the chemical's use, but all the studies concerning the effect of a chemical are based on that chemical and that chemical alone. The problem is that one chemical interacts with another and then another. They all are flushed into the sea or the water waste systems where the large contaminants are removed, but the chemicals combine on their own in a million random ways. If you tried to test just one thousand chemicals interacting with just three others in all possible combinations you would need to do more than a million tests. Even if you know for certain what the new life form will do in a sample of sea water you now have in your lab, that water would not be the same the next day if you took another sample in the exact same place."

"Toxic soup."

"Yes. Didn't you ever flush an expired prescription down the toilet? Where do you think those chemicals go? They don't die. They wash down the sewer to the treatment plant where they join thousands of other chemicals that were flushed down the drain, not to mention cleaners, pesticides, make up, and God knows what else, and they all end up in the water. You cannot say with any degree of conviction what is in the best-treated water, because no one can possibly test for all the substances that come into the system."

"OK, I'll agree with you there."

"Then the water supply is treated and the effluents are dumped into the rivers and carried to the sea where they meet with all the other chemicals from all the other cities and rivers and they combine on their own. Do people think they just float in layers and agree to stay away from each other? If I took out three things from our medicine cabinet and mixed them together and told you to drink it, would you?"

"Not on a bet."

Cassidy patted her tummy. "I've been thinking a lot about this because of little Francis."

"About the water?"

"About the state of life on Earth. I'm afraid to drink tap water and after what we learned was happening in America, I'm afraid to drink bottled water. I'm making myself crazy with all of this. I don't think I can keep my focus on it because I begin to see everything as toxic. I begin to view the world and every substance in it as toxic. If I try and eat only organic items, then I limit what I can eat and I cheat little Francis out of some things he needs to grow. However, if I give him non-organic things then I might be introducing him to toxic substances. It's enough to drive me crazy. I don't think people can live in constant anxiety about the environment and what it is doing to them."

"Cassidy, there is no plan to release this water in the oceans."

"You promise?"

"Yes. Maurice has assured me that he has a stringent protocol of containment."

"You don't know what people are capable of when money is the motive. Anyway, who's funding this project, Francis?"

"I, ah, well, the ESA, the European Space Agency, I presume."

"You don't know for sure?"

"I'm not absolutely certain. I assumed — "

'Hon, you might want to ask that question considering your last funding experience."

Chapter 16

"Mister Purlough, your son is on the line again."

Purlough grabbed the phone, "How's my little granddaughter doing?"

"It doesn't look good, dad. Her electrolytes are way off and she can't sustain hydration. They are certain that it was heavy water. They are thinking it was done by terrorists."

"You'll have to fly her here. I have access to some of the best doctors and minds in the world. I might even have a machine, a device I know of — "

"Dad, we can't move her."

"There must be something that can be done — "

"They are working on it night and day."

"Let me get this spiraling machine I put into storage last year."

"What on Earth are you talking about?"

"It cured a young woman I know. You have to get her here."

"They say she can't be moved."

"Don't argue with me, son. I know it sounds fantastic but the world within which I operate is full of fantastic things. I'll call you back in twenty minutes."

Alford Purlough hung up and dialed a number on a private cell phone he kept just for calls outside the knowledge of the Cartel. They bugged most of the high level employees' land lines and gave them cell phones they could trace.

"Hello, Donald?"

"Purlough, hold on — "

"Yes, I'll hold…"

"Hello, this is Donald."

"Alford here. The item I had shipped to you last year, is it available for immediate shipping?"

"It will take some work. I had to move it last month. Some people from the Cartel were sniffing around."

"Is it in country?"

"No, not exactly."

"Where then?"

"Shipping container at sea."

"How far out?"

"Six days."

"I'll send a helicopter for it."

"That won't work. The ship can't handle a copter."

"I told you to keep it available." Purlough's voice reflected his growing anger.

"You told me to deep six it. You didn't say anything about immediate retrieval."

"Donald, I need that shipment and I need it tomorrow."

"I'll call the ship and get an exact location. It may be near a port of call and we could possibly do a pick up."

"Call me in ten minutes."

Purlough dialed his son. The phone rang ten times before voice mail picked it up. Purlough hung up and hit redial. His son finally answered.

Before he could say anything, Purlough blurted out, "I have found the device. It may take a day or two."

"Dad, dad listen to me, you are too late."

"No. No, it will just take a day or two."

"Dad, you are not listening to me. It's too late. She's gone."

"Bastards!"

"Who?"

"Bastards! Son, listen to me. I think I know who did this."

"Did what? What do you mean?"

"I know who contaminated the water. Wait, we can't talk on this phone."

Chapter 17

Adam Halter walked around the lab. He disliked places he could not understand or control. His trip to France had been tiring, even in a private jet, and now after two meetings with individual Cartel members, he'd finally arrived in Paris at the lab. In his company were two men. They went with him wherever he traveled and provided a perimeter around him. Adam disliked people intensely and his men made sure he didn't have to deal with anyone other than those he wished to intimidate or seduce.

"Mister Adams, is it?" Flauneau greeted him.

"No. It is Mister Halter."

"How may I help you?"

"I'm about to help you."

"Oh?"

"I am about to secure funding for this project for the next two years."

"Wonderful."

"If."

"If what?"

"If you can assure me that no one is working on the project that is troublesome."

"Is this about Allenton, because if it is let me assure you that he is a first rate scientist and has been helpful already in — "

"You have given him access to the project?" Adam sneered at Maurice.

"He has made some preliminary examinations of the stellar water and helped with some observations of the sea water reactions."

"I thought we had made ourselves clear on this subject. Did you get a telephone call from Estan Milan?"

"Yes, but that was just last night."

"The conditions of our funding are quite clear, at least we presumed they were clear to Mister Milan. We say who works on this project."

"I was told by Purlough I would have a free hand."

"You were misinformed. Mister Purlough has become ill and unable to perform his duties. I am acting in his stead. I will be taking samples back to the States with me tomorrow."

"I have the greatest confidence in Doctor Allenton."

"Don't you have the picture yet? He is not going to work on this project. I can see you have an attachment to him. I was assured by Milan that you would not let your interest in men get in the way of your performance."

Standing up, Maurice said. "I resent your implications." As he stood the thuggish men that came into the lab with Adam moved in closer, arms across their chests.

"Resent what you will. I realize this situation has caused you some discomfort. Perhaps we can smooth this out. If you will give me his address, I will go by his home and made the necessary corrections this situation requires."

"I brought him on. It seems only decent that I should tell him."

"Yes, perhaps you are right. However, in concerns like this we like to pay a house call."

"It's hard to find."

"Perhaps we have not impressed upon you how important this decision is for us." Adam said as he moved within inches of Maurice's face.

Maurice jotted down an address and handed it to Adam. One of his men took it from Maurice.

"I'm looking forward to working with you, Maurice. You seem such a reasonable fellow." Adam stood and turned away from him. "I don't expect you will remember this conversation tomorrow."

"No. I have no memory of it now." Maurice said. Before the door had closed behind them, Maurice had picked up the telephone to call Francis.

Chapter 18

Alford Purlough cried. Silent tears ran down his cheek. He pushed them off with his hand. He had not allowed himself to feel his own humanity for many years. He was a man of stone, or so he thought. The death of his granddaughter at the hands of the Cartel sent a shiver of sobriety through him. He had been part of a group that historically had been ruthless, but they had always stopped short of harming children. True, they had killed people to take advantage of opportunities brought by the deaths, and true as well, they had robbed, lied and manipulated for their own gain. Marilee's was not a death, distant and vague, surrounded by the euphemisms masking and minimizing terrible acts, this was a death, close and difficult.

Purlough disliked what the Cartel had become. New people had brought a layer of evil that defied denial. The older members had only sanctioned elimination of individuals for a very specific reason. Now those highly placed people had begun to change as if the new wrapper around them held them in a grip of fear.

Purlough was well-placed and knew most of the secrets, all of the lies, some of the atrocities, and he suspected his illness now made him a target for elimination. On some levels he wondered if his illness was as innocent as the company doctor had made it out to be. He knew the Water Cartel had the ability to make people ill in a variety of ways.

Purlough turned over inside. The way a lake raises all the bile from the bottom and stands stagnant for a moment, then its new clean water rises to the surface. Purlough decided to set things straight while he still had the power to do so. He had no delusions of grandeur or reformation, he was a vengeful man and the Cartel, either as a whole or part, had wounded him. None who dared to do so in the past were still living. He felt he had a small window of opportunity through which to strike at those who had drawn blood from his family.

"I need a location on Adam Halter." He barked at his secretary.

"France." She said.

"That's a big country, I need a precise location."

He redialed a number reserved for special events. A voice answered.

"We need a carpet cleaned." He used a coded message. "A friend of mine hired you to clean one. The carpet belonged to a Dr. Lin."

"Yes, that one was cleaned by us."

"I presume the fee is the same." Purlough asked.

"The same. Do you have an address?"

The line rang from the secretary.

"Just one moment, please." Purlough motioned for the secretary to pick up the line. "Would you tell the gentleman the address I asked you to get for me?" He returned to the man on the phone. "My secretary has the address. I hope you will do as good a job as you did for my friend. The carpet belongs to Adam Halter. I believe I sent you a file on him a few months ago."

"You can be assured of the quality of our workmanship."

Purlough ran his hands across his address book. Picking up the phone he made another call to an associate at the University of Louisiana.

"Justin, I have an offer."

"Alford, nice to hear from you."

"I have funds for an endowed chair, but I have to have the man I want."

"The sponsorship of an endowed chair is long lasting. Are you prepared to make that level of commitment?" Justin asked.

"Yes."

"We aren't allowed to have the strong-handed control on them that we used to have. They are a lot more independent than in the past."

"No control. This is a farm out. Someone we want content for a long time."

"I see."

"I will have him contact you next month. His name is Allenton, Francis Allenton. He is a distinguished water scientist, a bit controversial perhaps."

"There is the new biology center fund raiser coming up in August. Did I tell you about it?"

"Extortionist. How much?"

"Some are giving as much as a hundred thousand."

"I'll get back to you on that. The endowment will be arranged by my lawyer. I'll have him get in touch."

Purlough hung up the telephone. Turning to his secretary he smiled and gathered a brief case from the floor.

"I'll be gone for three days."

"You have meetings back to back tomorrow." She protested.

"Tell them I'm sick."

The secretary made a scowl indicating her displeasure with his decision. "Is there anything I can do for you, sir?" she asked.

"I have already taken care of it. Thank you just the same. I have some family issues to resolve. I shall be back in three days. Be a good girl, will you, lie for me."

Chapter 19

The telephone produced a persistent and irritating ring. Francis and Cassidy sat still for a moment and enjoyed their little routine of mocking out the phone by making a similar irritating noise each time it rang. On the fourth ring Francis pulled himself from the overstuffed chair and picked up the receiver.

"Allenton here."

"Francis, this is Maurice."

"What have you got? Did something happen at the lab?"

"No, nothing like that. I want to talk to you about the project. Some things have come up here and I was just concerned…"

"Oh?"

"Do you have any reason to be worried about your safety?"

"Why?"

"Some men were just here, from the States. I didn't like them. They have your address. I think it might be a problem for you. I'm sorry I gave them your address, but they were most insistent."

"What men?"

Cassidy looked at Francis with concern.

"Men I didn't like. I don't mean to scare you, but you might want to leave. You can come to my home if you wish."

"What is he saying?" Cassidy asked.

"Some men came looking for me from the States." Francis told her. "Listen Maurice, don't feel bad about it. Thank you for calling. I'll get back to you tomorrow."

"That's the other thing. They said they didn't want you in the project."

"Who are they?"

"Funding people, you know. You must have really made someone very unhappy before you came to Paris."

"You could say that. Listen, I'm going to go. I'll call you."

"Call me at home." Maurice said and hung up.

"Cassy, honey, we need to go out."

The phone rang again. Neither of them made fun of the phone's ring this time.

"Hello?" Francis answered cautiously.

"Doctor Allenton, this is Alford Purlough."

"How did you get this number?"

"Never mind that. I can't explain myself right now, but I need you and your wife to leave home immediately. There is a man coming to see you, and you don't want to see him. I am going to deal with this, but you have to trust me."

"Not bloody likely." Francis told him.

"I can't explain now. There isn't time. They killed my grandchild. You have to get out of your home. I am going to give you a number and I want you to go to a public place and call me. You need to go now. Take your passports with you."

"Why should I believe you?" Francis asked.

"Yes, why indeed? You have no reason, but I am confident your life and the life of your wife are in danger. I'm not a good man, Doctor Allenton, but I'm not going to let them get away with this. You must leave. Please, you must leave. What is there to lose by going out and calling me?"

"I don't trust you, Purlough. You ruined my reputation."

"Yes. Yes. Now I am saving your life." Purlough gave him the number and hung up.

"What?" Cassidy asked.

"Purlough."

"You are shitting me."

"He says we should leave the house, right now."

"Why?"

"Men are coming for us."

"OK, let's go."

"You trust him?" Francis seemed confused.

"Well, I don't think he would have called to send us out into the night to an unknown destination. He has no way of knowing where we might go. If he was part of the danger, he would have nothing to gain by warning us. No, I think we should go and go right now."

The narrow streets absorbed Cassidy and Francis into their dark recesses. They walked toward a café three blocks away that was open late. Francis found a pay phone and called Purlough.

"OK, we're out."

"Good. Now, I am sending some funds to you, and they will be deposited into your account. Do not go back to your home. Whatever is there is not worth the peril of going back."

"Leave everything?"

"Yes. I will replace everything. Register at a hotel under an assumed name and leave for the States tomorrow. But first, go to your bank in the morning. I have it all in hand, but it will take a few days to calm things down. Call this number when you arrive in New York."

"I'll give you the bank account number." Francis told him as he pulled out his wallet.

"I know it. I'll send twenty thousand dollars as a measure of good faith."

"Twenty thousand?"

"Yes, as a show of good will. Additionally, I have the means to secure employment for you in the Gulf region."

"I won't work for the Cartel."

"You already do." Purlough informed Francis.

"I have a question, something to show your good faith as you say." Francis said.

"What?"

"Where is my Caduceus?"

"I have it. We will talk when you get here." Purlough hung up again.

"What are we to do?" Cassidy asked.

"We are to get a hotel room tonight, go to the bank in the morning to get some money, then immediately go back to the States. No matter what, we are not to go back to our place."

"You are kidding. What else did he say?"

"We have to return to the States. He says he can secure a job for me."

"You don't want to work for him, do you?"

"He said I am already working for him. He said he will explain it to us when we get back. He's sending money as a show of faith."

"Money doesn't buy my faith. It would take ten thousand dollars for me to trust that man."

"Well then, you will trust him twice. I have to call Maurice."

"Twice? Oh, Francis. Wait, call Maurice, do you think that is wise?"

"I trust him. I need to tell him we are leaving."

Francis dialed Maurice at home.

"Hello."

"Maurice?"

"No, this is Rene. Just a moment."

Francis scanned the streets outside the café. Nothing unusual seemed to be happening. He saw three men walking together. They appeared young and playful. He doubted they were the men Purlough warned against.

"Hello." Maurice answered.

"Maurice, this is Francis."

"Are you and your wife all right?"

"Yes, we had to leave the apartment. Listen, this is a little awkward. I have to return to the States, right away."

A long silence took over the conversation. It was an awkward moment for Francis who had come to like Maurice and trust him.

"Of course, Doctor Allenton. It has been a pleasure working with you and learning how you think."

"Don't be formal, Maurice."

"The situation calls for some formality, Doctor Allenton. I wish you and your new family well. I am quite unskilled in the fine art of endings. I find myself clumsy and saying things that sound insincere or trite. It is worth saying, however, that I admire you and perhaps under different circumstances we would have worked out a situation that was more stimulating."

"I have enjoyed working with you, Maurice. Please tell Rene that I wish you and him happiness."

"So I shall. Let's keep in touch."

"There is so much more I wanted to learn about the stellar water. I may have the opportunity to contact you in the future, after a few things get sorted out."

"I, too, was looking forward to greater discoveries. However, it was not to be."

"You will keep the water in the lab contained, won't you?"

"I'll do what I can. There is a man, he's taking some of the stellar water. I will do what I can."

"Well, until another day then." Francis said.

Maurice hung up the phone. He found himself with a lump in his throat. While Maurice did not openly admit to any feelings of affection toward Francis, he did allow himself to occasionally think of him in a romantic moment. He so disliked dishonesty. He turned to Rene with a pained expression.

"Are you all right, Sweetheart?" Rene asked.

"I'm fine. You know me, just an old softy."

"Don't go all drip about him, Maurice, you still have me."

"It's not like that." Maurice protested. "I had to let him go anyway."

"Let him go?"

"Yes, the money came calling today. They didn't want him on the project."

"So, it's all tidy then."

"Tidy? Yes, I guess you could say that."

"Fiddle dee dee. That's how life goes, isn't it." Rene made light of the situation not knowing the darker aspects of the group funding his partner's lab.

Across town Cassidy and Francis found a small hotel and checked in. They sat on a dilapidated bed and together with big sighs they fell back to stare at the ceiling.

"Don't you find this all a little deja vu?" Cassidy asked.

"In what sense?" Francis replied.

"I just mean out of the blue Purlough finds us and sends money for us to return to the States. I'm just saying it seems to fit together a little too neatly. First Purlough is against us and now he's our best friend and protector."

"You said we should trust him—the money, the warning — ."

"Yes, but, okay, letting it go — yes, I can feel it, there it goes, right out of my mind. All gone now." Cassidy made a pretend wipe of her hands.

"Feeling a little protective over me lately, are we?"

"Yes, you do have a history of being a little too trusting."

"I have a mother, thank you."

"A great one at that. She could have taught you a little more about being too trusting, however. No. No. There I go, letting it go, letting it go again." Cassidy returned to her pretended hand wiping.

"What seems out of the blue to you, may simply mean that I still have value to Purlough. I do have a reputation as a first rate water scientist."

"Yes, a well-deserved reputation. I'm not saying you don't deserve respect and opportunities. It's just when the wind blows and a tree falls I think they might be related, that's all."

"You know what, you're right. I'm gullible, but I would rather live my life believing in the goodness of things that happen to me rather than arm myself for the outrageous evils of my fellow man. It's a fault I have, you're right."

Cassidy lay still realizing she had stumbled into an area of Francis' vulnerability. She had not meant to drag up issues of Francis' character, but her efforts had become snagged like fish caught in a trawler's net. She had brought up an entirely different catch than intended.

She believed that their marriage was strong, but realized it had corners that were fragile. She knew that their relationship sometimes hit a hidden snag that didn't emerge until one or the other of them unintentionally brought it to the surface. Even if revealed by accident, that vulnerability remained exposed to the light of day. She had wounded Francis' pride by suggesting he was too trusting, but it had been his openness that had attracted her.

"I'm calling Maurice back." Francis said reaching for the phone.

"Why?" Cassidy had just started to the bathroom but stopped as she reached the door.

"I don't like how it ended, just kind of trailed off. He's a good man and a fine mind; he needs to know I respect him. He told me how he felt about me and I just kind of fumbled around."

"Do what you need to do then." Cassidy walked into the bathroom hoping her words showed support in some measure to reassure Francis about her trust of him. She heard Francis dial and then closed the bathroom door behind her.

"Allo!" a voice answered.

"Maurice?"

"No. He's gone back to the lab. May I help you?"

"This is Francis Allenton."

"Oh, the famous Doctor Allenton. I've heard much of you."

"Ah, Rene. I had something I wanted to say to Maurice."

"Well, Doctor Allenton, he's been in quite a snit today over it all."

"I'm sorry?"

"Perhaps it would be best if you just let things stand where they are. I'm certain he wouldn't tell you. That's the way he is, Maurice is a perfect gentleman."

"I see."

"No, I don't think you see the whole picture, but it doesn't matter. We all have our little fantasies."

"Will you tell him I called?"

"What's the point, Doctor? You're history as far as he is concerned."

"I didn't like how things were left. I wanted to let him know that I admired his work."

"Don't encourage him. He's very tired. Could I ask you to just let things stand as they are?"

"I'm not very comfortable with that just now."

"You don't understand him like I do. Don't tease him with flattery. I know what that will do to him. It will just keep him pining away for more."

"I don't understand." Francis found himself in a conversation about Maurice's character instead of talking to Maurice about his admiration of his talents.

"You never will. Let's just let this go, shall we?"

Rene hung up abruptly.

Cassidy walked in as Francis slowly laid the phone back in its cradle. "How did it go?" she asked.

"Oh, famously I should say, famously."

"Everything all right?"

"Everything is fine. We are hiding in a cheap hotel in Paris. I have been thrown out of the stellar water project. Some men are looking for me that I would rather not meet. We are going back to the states under the care and protection of the first and only real enemy I ever had. Yes, all and all, I would say my career has peaked."

They were both quiet. Cassidy stretched out, lost in thought, and still worried about her decision to trust Purlough.

Francis spoke softly, "Cassidy, sorry, I forgot to tell you something. Purlough said he has the Caduceus."

"Oh, Francis, really?"

Chapter 20

The temperature outside was near one hundred. The moist Gulf air hung heavy. Francis was happy to leave it outside when they entered the doctor's office. The waiting room was hectic. The phone rang without being answered and two young children were playing in a toy corral. Francis sat stiffly as two small children began yelling and throwing bright plastic toys at each other. A child with a head cold handed him a plastic duck wet with drool. Francis smiled uncomfortably at him, taking the duck between two fingers and placing it on the floor. The child bent over and tried to place it in his hands. Cassidy discouraged the child briefly with a stern look, but he soon returned his attention to Francis.

"He likes you." She told Francis.

"Lucky me."

"I suppose it's too late to change our mind about children." Cassidy teased, patting her large belly.

"Don't even." Francis sighed and gave her a look, one part exasperation and ten parts admiration.

Since they had relocated to the lower Gulf area, Francis had started his job as principal investigator for the University and they had retrieved their furniture and other belongings left behind in storage when they moved to Paris. Now they had begun to settle into a routine. Being in the States was comforting with Baby Francis on the way. In addition, they realized that a lot of French culture maintained itself in the southern Louisiana Gulf area. Unfortunately, Francis found the Cajuns as hard to understand as Cassidy had found the French. The natives talked rapidly and at times it seemed to him that they must have mouths full of crawfish.

The doctor's visit was prompted by Cassidy having some difficulties. She attributed them somewhat to their abrupt departure from Paris and all of the moving adjustments they had been through, but she also had a premonition of trouble. She had that ability, to sense trouble before it came to the surface. Weeks before she was diagnosed with cancer, she had a feeling that something was amiss within.

"It isn't anything I can put my finger on," she had told Francis, "just a feeling that we better go check things out." Francis had picked up the phone and made the appointment within minutes of her pronouncement. He had come to trust her intuition, even more, perhaps, than she.

A couple sitting across from them squabbled. She was a tiny, dark-haired woman and he was a robust, bald man. They acted like they both ached for relief from each other's company. The woman tried to start a conversation with Cassidy.

"First baby?" she asked.

"First of ten." She answered watching out of the corner of her eyes to gauge Francis' reaction. He stiffened more. She thought if he stiffened his legs further he would end up standing.

When they finally were called to see the doctor and rose to follow the nurse, the boisterous children quickly took over Francis' seat playing a kind of guns and robbers game. They had been playing with such realism that Francis wondered if they were reenacting events they had seen in their neighborhood.

"Ours won't be like that." Cassidy said in a reassuring tone when they walked toward the exam room.

Francis gave her one of his funny smiles that had a habit of turning down at the edge of his mouth. It began as a smile but as it emerged, as often as not, the smile turned into a sardonic grimace. She asked him about it once or twice but it made him feel self-conscious. The only exception was when she caught him off guard and would make a funny face or tickle him, then his turned-up-corners-of-the-mouth smile emerged. She loved that one as it was clear to her what it meant. The sardonic smile face was still a puzzle. That was the one he wore into the doctor's office.

Cassidy went behind the curtain pulled around by the nurse and slipped into the obligatory gown and laid the paper sheet over her legs. She pulled back the curtain and gave Francis a smile and started to say something to him when the door opened.

"Well, what seems to be troubling you, Mrs. Allenton?" the doctor began.

"I seem to be reacting to everything. I get blotchy skin and itch when I come into contact with plastic or latex or anything artificial."

"I see. Have you had this kind of reaction before?"

"No."

"Asthma?"

"No."

"Any diseases? I'm not sure this intake form is correct, it says cancer."

"I had a brief scare with cancer some time ago. It seems gone now."

"Radiation?"

"No, just water." Cassidy gave Francis a knowing look.

"Water? That's a new one. Well, let's have a look at this irritation."

Francis leaned back and looked at the tiles on the ceiling as Cassidy lifted her exam gown and the doctor looked at her upper torso.

"I don't think it is anything too serious. I'm confident it won't affect the baby. I'm guessing a contact dermatitis, maybe some kind of chemical sensitivity. I could give you some allergy pills."

"I'm not sure, with the baby and all."

"This drug is safe enough, but okay, let's try oatmeal baths. Can't be too careful at this stage of pregnancy, can we?" The doctor smiled at Francis and Cassidy stifled a giggle as she realized that totally unaware, Francis was leaning back with his head resting on the lower end of a poster with a detailed drawing of a woman's gynecological anatomy.

"What? Oh, yes, I always prefer natural solutions when at all possible." Cassidy was sure the doctor had no clue what was funny.

"Keep an eye on it, will you, and get back to me if it worsens. On another issue, Mrs. Allenton, your age places you in the high risk pregnancy category, and your Rh factor also gives us concern. We will need to have a neonatal specialist in the delivery room. Some tests may need to be done on the baby at that time, but everything is looking fine today."

"What are the odds that we will need to do a C-section?" Cassidy asked.

"Perhaps as many as thirty percent of high risk mothers have C-sections."

"Let's take every possible precaution necessary. It's taken me my whole life to have this baby and I want to plan ahead."

Cassidy dressed and they left the office.

"I didn't know you had allergies." Francis said.

"What?" Cassidy asked.

He pushed open the door for her and they felt the whoosh of the hot humid air rush over them.

"Chemical sensitivity, isn't that what the doctor said?" Francis held her arm as they walked.

"I knew a nurse back in Missouri that reacted to gloving. When she was near latex of any type she would break out. I told her it was Mother Nature's revenge, getting us back for making all these chemicals. Well, I'm not sure what caused mine. I've seen a lot on the internet lately about people who cannot even go out in the environment anymore. They seem to be allergic to everything."

"What was your question about a C-section?" Francis seemed anxious.

"Just planning ahead. You know me. Everything will be fine. Don't worry." Cassidy decided to keep her humorous observation of Francis to herself.

They walked to the car talking about Baby Francis and enjoying the beauty of the billowing clouds that gave them a break from the heat of the sun.

Chapter 21

Adam had arrived in the Gulf. He disliked the sea because it was raw and unfettered. He had brought from France a special container filled with a mixture that sustained the ravenous radiolaria. One of the two men with Adam held the container as the three of them stood on the platform floating in the dead zone. The scientist who worked there daily, stood watching. A plastic barrier floated around the platform to form a containment area.

Today the oceans were heavy following a storm in the Gulf and waves rolled over the sides of the containment area.

"Waves are too rough today, Mister Halter." The scientist warned.

"Do you know what day it is today?" Halter asked.

"Yes."

"No, I don't think you do. Today is the day that you are going to start looking for a new job."

"But, sir, the protocol on containment is very clear. We are not to put the sample in the containment area when the seas are rough. The waves are both coming in and going out of the area."

"You, sir, are too timid to work for me." Adam approached the container. He signaled for his men to continue. "Dump this water!"

"Wait!" The scientist yelled. The two men took the container and dumped it in the ocean.

"You see?" Adam responded. "There isn't anything I want to happen that doesn't happen."

When Alford Purlough learned Adam had left France for the Gulf, he quickly called the cleaners again.

"Yes?"

"I was expecting to hear from you concerning the appointment I made with you."

"That carpet has been very difficult to locate. The address you gave us was not valid."

"I was under the impression that you could find it easily."

"The carpet in question is difficult to find."

"I have a more solid address for you today. It is in Louisiana. The carpet in question has become quite soiled. We are most anxious to have it cleaned."

"We will do our best."

Purlough was irritated. He had begun to feel a burning sensation across his torso. The company doctor told him it may be allergies, but Purlough knew his skin had an infection that was a serious threat to his health. The Caduceus, created by Francis to spiral spring water into healing water awaited Purlough, but he was uncertain how to make it work.

"Call for you, Doctor Allenton." The secretary at the front of the building yelled in her deep Louisiana drawl.

Francis thought her pronunciation of "you" seem longer than three letters. "Dorene, try to use the intercom, please." He yelled back.

The secretary pushed the button to activate the intercom, but the phone's technology continued to escape her. "Oh dear, I'm afraid I have lost him, Doctor. No, wait, here he is."

"Never mind, Dorene, I'll come up." Francis took off a pair of protective glasses and moved from his lab table to the desk phone with two lines blinking.

"Which one, Dorene? Dorene! Which line is it?"

"The blinking one."

"There are two blinking."

"Oh, now see, you've got me confused again, Doctor. Number two, yes, I'm certain."

Francis pushed the first button. "Hello."

"Allenton?"

He recognized the voice instantly, "Yeah."

"This is David."

"Yes, David. How are you? We have been meaning to call you since we got back."

"You're a hard man to find, Allenton. I'm in the area. I have to talk to you. Would you and Cassidy join me for lunch tomorrow?"

"Well, she's been feeling a little under the weather lately."

"She's all right, isn't she?"

"Yes, just some allergies we think."

"Hell, it's no wonder we don't all swell up and die with the air and water like it is. Come on, I'll pay."

"You'll pay?"

"I've got grant money, buddy, a bucket of it. You won't believe it, just bam, out of the blue, and I'm talking real money here."

"To do what?"

"That's what I want to talk to you about. Come on. Lunch up at Praleen's. You know where it is?"

"Yeah, up by the highway."

"Noon or so tomorrow?"

"Fine. I'll talk to her. Give me your number in case she's not feeling well."

"Come on, Doc, you're not jealous, are you?"

"No, really, she's been sick."

"Well, get yourself up here for lunch. I've got a lot to tell you."

David gave Francis his cell phone number and hung up. Francis had to admit he didn't like him much. David hadn't really done anything to make him dislike him, but Francis was certain that the friendship between Cassidy and David in college was more than platonic. He'd just rather not think about it.

Cassidy agreed to have Francis pick her up for lunch with David. Perhaps she was curious or perhaps she wanted to show David her relationship with Francis since it had been David who had ended theirs. She had been wounded by David's rejection. Now, years later, she was happy and successful and she didn't mind letting him get a glimpse of the woman she had become.

The restaurant was busy. On stage a zydeco band played Cajun music, then the band members moved down among the tables and tourists got up to follow them through the aisles in a half march, half dance. Cassidy and Francis retreated to stand near a stuffed alligator at least twelve feet long while they waited for their table. Some patrons milled about looking at T-shirts and curios until their number was called. Servers passed by with piles of freshly fried seafood, alligator tails, and hush puppies on large dark trays.

David arrived twenty minutes late. He was well-dressed in belted Bermudas and a freshly laundered polo shirt instead of the ragged shorts and torn Green Peace T-shirt that he had worn the first time Francis met him. He had let his hair grow out and had pulled it into a tiny pony tail. He wore a small diamond earring.

Cassidy noticed Francis stiffen as they shook hands. David turned to Cassidy and embraced her. She hugged him and patted him formally on his back.

"Cassy, God, it's good to see you. Just look at you. All dressed up with your big lady clothes on. Pregnant as a Puffin!"

"David, it's good to see you again." Cassidy trying to keep the exchange tight and formal.

"Hell, you're getting as big as a barn. Pregnancy agrees with you."

"Thank you. You look well."

"Success will do that to you."

"Francis said you were working with grant money." Keeping her eyes on David, Cassidy moved closer to Francis when she spoke and slipped her hand into his.

"Yes, finally have enough money to live well. I even replaced the old bug. Got a new one though, some things a radical leftover hippie shouldn't change."

"You got rid of Gertrude?" Cassidy said recalling the name of the old Volkswagen.

"No, not really. I'm having her restored."

A rotund woman called, "Allenton party of three" and they were seated near the bar. It was noisy as the band had begun another song with lots of rebel yells in it. After they ordered, Francis turned his attention to David's purpose of the meeting.

"Well, what's up David?" Francis asked.

"I thought you might know what's going on out at that platform I took you to see earlier.

"I'm not on that research project anymore, not since we came back to the States."

"Well, my research project is a detailed mapping of the dead zone. The grant specified the longitude and latitude of the measurements and the platform is dead in the middle."

"I'm not aware of any activity. My research is looking into algae life cycles in the Gulf dead zone."

"Algae?"

"Yes."

"That's curious."

"Curious?" Francis leaned forward.

"I'm getting some extraordinary findings about the algae."

"How so?"

"I'll tell you, but I want this kept at the table. I'm seeing a decline in the algae for no apparent reasons."

"Isn't that counter intuitive?" Cassidy asked. She had been watching Francis and David talk. She sensed some similarities. Both were intense when focused on their causes. Both had a kind of boyish appeal and both wore their vulnerabilities close to the surface.

"Yes." David and Francis answered in unison.

"I thought the algae bloom was the main reason for the dead zones." Cassidy continued. "Isn't that the reason the lower strata sea life die, too much algae? What would account for the reduction of the algae colonies?"

"I don't know." David said. He turned to Francis. "Do you?"

"I might. It depends on what they are doing out there, but I might know how the algae are being removed."

"Well, give it up, man." David leaned toward Francis.

"Predation."

"By what?"

"By a zooplankton."

"Not a lot of zooplankton eat algae." David looked at both of them.

"Especially not algae found naturally in the Gulf." Francis went on.

"And by found naturally you mean indigenous to the Gulf?"

"Yes, that's precisely what I mean."

"You really do know something about this, don't you?" David asked. He turned to face only Cassidy, "He knows something, doesn't he, Cassy?"

Cassidy turned her attention toward her bread stick. She didn't want to reveal any secrets to David although she knew David was a stronger environmental activist than Francis and would know what to do if the predatory zooplankton had been released into the Gulf.

David's distress was showing in his flushed face, "I can't believe it. Francis, if you know something that they are doing out there on that platform you need to tell me."

"I don't know anything."

"Well, if you don't know, then you do suspect something."

"I suspect a lot of things. I am a scientist. I don't deal in suspicion."

"Don't clam up on me, Francis. What's happening out there?"

"I don't know."

Cassidy turned to Francis, but while she looked at him, she spoke to David. "David, would you give Francis and me a moment alone at the table. Go powder your nose or something."

David rose from the table nearly spilling his water glass. He threw his napkin on his plate and sauntered up some nearby steps heading towards the restroom.

"Francis, Sweetheart, this is important, isn't it?"

"Yes."

"Do you think the rapidly evolving creatures you told me about have been introduced into the Gulf?"

"I don't know."

"But you suspect it is so."

"Yes. They are aggressive predators of the algae."

"Damn it all. Do you think they would put something like that in the sea?"

"If it would lead to a biotechnology they could sell, yes I do."

"Didn't you tell them about containment and possible spread?"

"Yes, I did, but my voice didn't count much with them."

"Perhaps that is why they wanted you out."

"You think they wanted me out of the way?"

"Well, your voice of caution has been silenced."

"Yes, I see, but here I am in the middle of the action. If they wanted to keep me out of it, the job Purlough arranged for me would have been in the Arctic or the Great Lakes or the Pacific. They brought us right here in the middle of it all."

"Do you know who funded your position?"

"No."

"Do you think we need to know?"

"Based on what David has told us, yes."

"Can you find out?"

"Maybe."

"What are you going to tell David?"

Francis piled his napkin on top of his plate, perhaps so as not to be outdone by David's flair. He pulled his glasses from his eyes and rubbed the area between them vigorously.

"I don't know anything. I'm not sure I'm ready to take him on as a partner."

Cassidy sensed jealousy. She had hoped the nature of the past relationship with David would be inconsequential, but now she was certain Francis was anxious about David.

"It's important, Francis. He needs to know if a new species has been introduced to the Gulf."

"To what gain?"

"He would take samples and ring the alarm if it is true."

"He wouldn't know what to look for."

"You do."

"Yes, I do."

"Do you need some time to decide?"

"Yes, I'm not certain."

Cassidy could see that David had emerged from the restroom and was hanging back in the distance like a child who was sent to his room and desperately wants to be allowed back. Francis saw him and waved for him to return to the table.

"All the family problems worked out now?" David asked in a flippant tone.

Cassidy cringed and thought he, too, sounded jealous.

Francis spoke as David sat down, "I'm going to do some of my own research into this issue. I will either do it alone or with your help. If I involve you, it will have to be done my way."

"I'm sorry, Doctor," David's tone was sarcastic. "I don't do anything using somebody's way."

David rose from the table. He turned and smiled at Cassidy. "Talk some sense into him, will you?"

After David walked away, Cassidy and Francis finished their lunch without speaking.

When they were through, Cassidy spoke first, "He's right, you know."

"Yes, Cassidy, I know David is right—just gripes my ass. That's all."

"Because?"

"Because you and him, I mean back then, I guess."

"Francis, please, don't waste your time on that."

Chapter 22

Francis was brushing his teeth. Neither he nor Cassidy had talked much the rest of the day. Cassidy had learned it was best to leave Francis alone to think when tension came between them.

"Do you know anything about tritium?" he asked her as if they had been having open communication all along.

"Why? Is that what's in your toothpaste?"

"God, I hope not. No, it's a radioactive substance found in heavy water and in extraterrestrial water."

"What does it do?"

"Like most radiation, it is mutagenic."

"Causes mutations, you mean?"

"Yes, or from another perspective, causes evolution. That is, of course, another explanation for evolution, creatures mutate or change in such a way that the change is successful and reproduced in the offspring."

"The algae eating creatures are mutations?" Cassidy asked. She knew he would not get around to talking about the Gulf if she didn't press him.

"Evolved perhaps, it is a fundamentally more advanced form of zooplankton than we had seen in the natural order of things. I think this is what is eating the algae in the dead zone. The experiments we did in France when we introduced the stellar water to the dead zone samples produced radiolaria, a kind of advanced form of zooplankton that is predatory on algae."

"How did they get into the water? Were they in the star water?"

"I'm not sure. My theory is they are there in the oceans in a suspended state."

"I don't follow you exactly."

"Do you remember how we moved into our old house and cleared the backyard of all the weeds and overgrowth, yet in the spring all the plants emerged. We didn't plant a single one of them and there they were."

"Yes, poison ivy and all."

"The seeds lay dormant in the soil until the conditions were right for them to emerge. I think the sea is like that. Life forms lie dormant in the sea until conditions are right to seed their growth."

"Aren't there radiolaria in the sea already?"

"They were present in the Cambrian."

"Where is the Cambrian sea?" Cassidy asked. She shuffled into the bathroom, her pregnant stomach pushing her robe open in the middle.

She constantly fussed with her clothes, partially from discomfort and occasionally from embarrassment at having such a large belly.

"Not where, but when. I meant the Cambrian as in the Cambrian Era."

"You mean these little creatures were alive in the Cambrian times, when life on Earth exploded, those Cambrian times?"

"Yes."

"What are you saying? Are you saying that the radiolaria are a result of someone seeding the oceans?"

"Yes."

"My God, how could they?"

"Profit. The world will pay heavily for a process that will clean the oceans of the algae blooms and return the dead zones to productive fishing waters."

"Biotechnology! How do they know what the Earth will do in response?"

"They don't know."

"What if Mother Nature makes a countermove and produces algae smarter than the predator?"

"Not likely, algae are plants."

"Not likely, haven't we talked about the development of plants that are able to avoid predation by deception or other methods?"

"Well, that's different. This is a single cell plant."

"That learned to live in a column of other single cell plants for protection."

"What are you saying? Are you serious that Mother Nature will find some way to defeat the radiolaria?"

"I'm saying that the need to survive is paramount and rather than be breakfast for the radiolaria, the algae will find a way to adapt, mutate, or evolve. It's the way of nature to find a way to survive rather than become extinct. This is bad, Francis, very bad. You really think they seeded the Gulf?"

"I do, as an experiment perhaps, but if they did, they could not contain it in a fixed area. The sea's currents move around the Earth. Some radiolarian will move in those currents. Others will be taken up in the moisture and redistributed across the Earth in the rains. Some radiolarian will attach themselves to the feet of birds or ride the skins of whales, but they will not be contained. I warned them in France about containment. I really did warn them."

"You have to tell David."

"I don't think he will know what to do. We are talking about a change of global proportion, and I don't think David is up to it."

"He's not stupid. He loves the Earth, it's something special about him."

"He's a radical. Who will listen to him?"

"You and David could try together. It's important, Francis. We don't know what will happen. It may already to too late to keep it under control. Mother Nature may rise up and try to fix this and the consequences may be catastrophic. There is nothing quite like an angry mother trying to protect her offspring. Believe me. I know something about this now. I used to be a pacifist, but just let someone threaten little Francis. I would kill to protect my child. I didn't understand that kind of protectiveness until now. Now that I have a baby inside me, I understand how far I would go to protect my offspring. The Earth Mother must be as protective. There might not be anything we can do now. She might be angry and righteously so."

"Gaia again?"

"Yes, Gaia, Mother Earth, Mother Nature, whatever you wish to call her, she is rising to protect herself from mankind. You have to call David. We have to let the world know what has happened in the Gulf."

Chapter 23

Francis reluctantly called David. He wasn't sure what to do, but he didn't wish to defy Cassidy or make little of her concerns. He knew she was probably right.

"David, this is Francis. We have to talk."

"I'll say. Do you know a man named Alford Purlough?"

"I do. Why?"

"He's your benefactor and it seems he is mine, too."

"Purlough? How do you know this?"

"One thing about Green Peace, Francis, you learn how to smell out the rats. One of my many jobs for them was finding out who really owned what. I learned to look behind fictitious companies to find the real owners of the polluting factories and other businesses. I started to ask myself how and why we both ended up in the Gulf area and how we both have highly funded projects that crossed paths. I don't hold much to coincidence."

"You think we are both in the Gulf by Purlough's design?"

"I know it. This Purlough guy grew up in the bayous south of New Orleans. He grew fat on oil money and owns a lot of land down here. He is an avid sportsman and works in Washington for some water group. He is a Sherpa for the G8 group so he has a lot to do with their policies concerning water quality, water policy, and waste management. I put in a call to his office and left a message."

"That might not be such a good idea."

"Too late, buddy. I called and left the message a half hour ago."

Francis held his hand over the phone while David was still talking. Cassidy gave him a questioning look. He mouthed words to her, "Water Cartel. Purlough. David knows."

"Purlough?" she mouthed back. He shook his head vigorously up and down.

"Listen, David, let me interrupt you. I've got some information about the Gulf and the algae, but I don't want to talk on the phone. Can you come by?"

David continued to talk as Francis tried to continue. "Purlough is a heavy hitter, I can tell you that. He's got money, too. Do you know him?"

"We met once in Washington."

"Good blood or bad blood between you and him?"

"Well, that's a difficult call. He may have saved our lives in Paris."

"Shit-o-la! Damn! What were you up to over there?"

"It's history or so I thought." Francis made more faces at Cassidy.

She put her hands in the air as if gesturing him to go forward. "So listen, David, the Gulf platform might be part of a project I was involved with in France."

"France? Are they doing research on the dead zones?"

"No, it was something else. Can we talk directly about this?"

"Yeah, wait, can you hold on? I got a call coming in — " the line went quiet.

"What's he saying?" Cassidy insisted.

"He's got another call." Francis continued to talk to Cassidy making large exaggerated silent pronunciations.

"OK, I'm back. Holy shit, man, that was Purlough. He wants a meeting."

"With?"

"You and me and Cass. Is this a good thing or a bad thing, Francis?"

"I don't know."

"If he is the boogeyman, then why give us money?" David asked.

"We need to meet him." Francis covered the phone again and told Cassidy. "Purlough wants to meet."

"Maybe it's time." Cassidy responded, "We certainly need to know why he has changed."

"What? Are you crazy?" Francis protested Cassidy's idea.

"Not as crazy as it may seem. You have to trust me on this. He saved us in Paris. He is up to something and my gut tells me we need to meet with him."

"Children, children," David was yelling into the phone. "Stop arguing. I'll set up the meeting."

"I don't want Cassidy there." Francis told David.

"Man, don't you know by now where Cass wants to go, she goes." David waited a moment, then spoke more softly, "I'll call you back with the details of the meeting." He hung up.

Francis hung up. "He's going to set up a meeting. I don't think this is a good idea, I mean, you going to see Purlough in your condition."

"I have every right to be there. Don't you dare try and stop me." Cassidy made angry eyes at Francis.

Chapter 24

The meeting place was at the water's edge. Alford Purlough stood beside a long sleek Lincoln and leaned against the trunk looking at the Gulf. Gulls swarmed above him as if they expected him to throw bread into the air. They turned gracefully in the air as if one wing were pinned to the blue sky.

Francis, David and Cassidy emerged from the new Volkswagen Beatle convertible. They approached Purlough with caution.

As he walked toward them, they saw his face with its dark, red blotches and his bandaged hands.

"You will excuse my appearance. The doctors say it is multiple chemical sensitivity. It makes me weak and dizzy, among other things. I stay at home a lot now and isolate myself. It gives me time to think, too much time I'm afraid."

"Good morning, Alford." David greeted him informally.

Purlough seemed to ignore him. "Look at that sky. Isn't it beautiful? There isn't anything like the Gulf in the morning. I grew up not far from here. My father was a fisherman and a farmer, but he loved this land and he loved the Gulf. We spent many days in a small fishing boat."

"You asked to see us." David broke the nostalgic moment.

"Yes. Yes, indeed. I wanted to tell you a story. A story about a man who was pulled away from the things he loved and found himself part of a process larger than he could control."

"The Cartel?" Francis asked.

"Yes, the Cartel and the G8 and other things too large to understand and too dangerous to know more about. Recently I have begun to realize just how ruthless these people are. They have proven themselves to be capable of unspeakable acts of cruelty to get what they want. They have always paid me well and I fancied myself part of their inner circle, but I was wrong. I was liked as long as I helped them, but when I began to show signs of weakness and became ill, they started to isolate me. More than that, however, I learned that the new people they brought in are cut from a different cloth, a cloth that has too much blood on it. I began to be relegated to the backside of the board room, but I still had power because I knew too much to be expendable and had too much they still wanted. I made sure of that. Less than a year ago they deeply hurt me. Perhaps it was accidental, perhaps by design, but they took something from me that I loved. I decided I had to find a way to get even."

"That's where we come in?" Cassidy caught his meaning.

"Yes, young woman. I was always impressed with your style and intelligence. You are a lucky man, Francis. She's a real prize." Alford turned to address Cassidy directly, "Perhaps more than any of the men gathered here today, you understand what's at risk. You understand how precious a life should be."

"The whole of the Earth is at stake," she said repeating softly, "the whole of the Earth."

"When I left the bayou and went to college, I didn't really believe in much of anything. Now, since the years have passed and I have grandchildren, I have begun to see the tragedy of the past in terms of the cost to the future." Purlough bent over and drew a circle in the sand. "When my granddaughter sweet Marilee died in Quebec because of their actions, I realized that it was too late for me to make the changes I wanted to make. Too late for one that I loved before greed swept her away.

Cassidy and Francis looked at each other. "Quebec." She whispered.

Purlough did not seem to notice. "It may be too late for all of you as well. I knew I had to do something. I knew that I could not continue to support the Cartel. Standing here by the Gulf, I sense of something coming this way. I can't put my finger on it, a great calamity, perhaps rising from the sea, the hand of the Earth pushing us away from the shore."

"It's never too late." David tried to enter the conversation, but Alford kept his focus on Cassidy.

She felt his intensity. His focus was like that of her dying patients when she was a hospice nurse. It was focus that needed a voice. Purlough's resolve came from a man who had lived recklessly and been hurt deeply. She understood impending death and the need to make a reckoning before the ability was lost. She had considered her own death in a new way when she was diagnosed with breast cancer. Some awaiting death want to right wrongs and others want to wrong those who have hurt them, but most are haunted by a dogged sense of determination. Purlough was a driven man.

"You see it, don't you, my child? The Earth is rising up against us all. The global warming, the pollution, toxic air; we have done damage to our source of life and now she is simply protecting her child. She is rising up, even now as we speak, to throw us from her back like we would pinch off a tic."

"Gaia knows what to do." Cassidy held his gaze.

"There is too much at stake. I have a son and one remaining grandchild. That one must not be taken from me. I know I've had a hand in this mess, but hasn't everyone? Who hasn't stood by and let their desire for comfort destroy the future?"

"Amen to that." David said.

"Did they seed the Gulf?" Francis interrupted.

Purlough turned to Francis, "It started as a containment project. Your words were heeded, Doctor Allenton. Maurice tried to enforce the containment. However, there is this man, Adam is his name, the man I warned you about in Paris. He was responsible for the test in the Gulf and the bio-boundary was insufficient to hold the mutations. The entire area has been infiltrated. I tried to put a safety net in place. I wanted people in place to take action before it got out of hand, but it spread exponentially, much wider than the computer models predicted."

"Why would the Cartel fund us?" Francis asked. "We are against everything they stand for."

"Francis, it was my personal money. I wanted you here as a safeguard. I knew you would find the mutated predators or if not you, David would find them. I set the conditions of your endowment and his grants in such a way that you two could discover what was happening. My timing — I fear it is too late. I have lost power within the Cartel. Adam has grown strong. I have been unable to neutralize his activities."

Turning back to face Cassidy, Purlough continued, "You, of all of us, you must understand what She is planning." He held out his bandaged right hand to Cassidy, "You as a mother, you must know what we should do. I must not lose another grandchild."

"The Earth will survive." Cassidy acknowledged her kinship with the Earth Mother. "She will find a way to rid herself of mankind or find a way to neuter the effects we are having. Perhaps she will limit our numbers by making sure we can no longer reproduce or perhaps a cataclysmic event or pestilence will reduce our numbers by the millions, but she will find a way to reduce our negative impact."

"Did she give me this curse?" Purlough exposed his blistering skin to Cassidy. "Is she responsible for the wave of illness sweeping the nation? We must stop her."

Cassidy stepped forward and gently took his hand in both of hers. "We cannot."

Francis stepped toward them. "What would you have us do?"

Purlough looked at him. "Make them aware. Sound the alarm. You and David and Cassidy must warn the world that a storm is coming. A storm of human misery such as the Earth has never seen."

"Who would believe me, a discredited water scientist? Thanks to you, I might add."

"Francis, I discredited you to save you. I knew I would need you. I have been the hand at your back and the money in your pocket. I was afraid this day would come. You need to help now. To insure your cooperation I have something to offer you."

"You ruined my reputation." Francis was provocative.

"Yes, that is true but it was either that or let them remove you like Doctor Lin."

"The Cartel did kill Lin."

"I saved you, Francis, and now your alliance with David and the determination of your wife will sound the alarm. It's not too late. My grandchild and your own unborn child need you to sound the alarm. I will not live much longer. Multiple chemical sensitivity is the least of my worries. I am terminally ill. I am not certain how long I shall live. It's not too late for the next generation. I hoped I could trust you and now the future depends on you. I have something I knew you would value as a sign of good will between us. Francis, I have your Caduceus."

"You what? Where?" Francis nearly shouted.

"It's in a safe place. I will give it to you when you have done what I have asked. I need it to help me. I won't live forever, but you might be able to give me enough strength to redeem myself."

Purlough reached into his coat then handed David a cell phone. "Use this to call me but only after ten at night and only on this phone. My number is in the memory code as number one."

Purlough turned once again to face the Gulf. The light of the evening sun had turned the small waves golden. Gulls flew and dipped their wings to the water. Past the breaking waves a fish leaped into the air. Cassidy thought Purlough looked small against the panoramic vastness of the Gulf. He raised him arms toward the water. Then lowering his arms, slowly moved to his car, climbed in and with a slight nod of his head, drove off.

As soon as Purlough's car began to move away, David looked at Cassidy, "What on Earth was that all over his body?"

"Multiple chemical sensitivity syndrome. It's been identified since the early 1940's, but the last I read on-line, it has affected tens of thousands of Americans. I did some research on it several years ago for the hospice group I worked with — we had a few people suffering from it."

"What causes it?" Francis asked. They had reached the convertible and Cassidy waited for Francis to get in the back so she could sit in the front seat where she was more comfortable.

"That's controversial. Some say it is psychosomatic, caused by stress, guilt, or psychological factors. Others say it is caused by repeated exposure to chemicals, particularly man-made or synthetic chemicals derived from oil and plastics. The problem is, we don't understand why exposure to nontoxic levels of chemicals would bring it on. Some think it may be many chemicals interacting with other chemicals and then with the individual that's unknowingly sensitive."

"Is it fatal?" David asked as he slid behind the wheel and started the car. "He looks pretty sick."

"It can be. For the most part there is wide disagreement concerning the best approach to treat it. In fact, it is one of the few syndromes in which the patients try to identify the sources of their own illness. There is even disagreement about what to call it. Some call it environmental illness, others call it chemical AIDS. Terms such as Twentieth Century Illness, total allergy syndrome, sick building syndrome, chemophobia and immune dysregulation have been used."

"In other words, nobody knows what causes it." Francis added.

David tapped his forehead. "I remember now, it's the environment's revenge illness we talked about years ago. Depression and anxiety go with it, isn't that right, Cassy?"

"That right, David." Cassidy shifting about in the seat. "At one time some referred to it as increased neurobiological sensitivity to chemicals in the environment. It was talked about for a few years after Toxic Shock Syndrome became widely known in the media, but eventually people began to ignore it. It was regarded as hysterical or self-produced symptoms and put aside as a psychological illness."

"What was Purlough asking us to do?" Francis asked.

"He thinks Mother Earth is rising up to rid herself of mankind. He wants us to warn the world to stop what it is doing. He wants us to tell the world about the mutated zooplankton and raise the alarm."

"Christ, Cassy, environmentalists have been screaming this message for thirty years now. Nobody listens or the few that do want to send a few dollars to reduce their guilt while they still consume products and have lifestyles that deplete the planet. The message is already out there. It is only through extremism and high profile incidences that we even get in the newspapers. We have been relegated to the fringe of society as radicals or eco-terrorists. Nobody wants to change or if they do, they are just a few affluent households separating their garbage into recycle containers. The message doesn't work."

Cassidy, Francis and David sat quietly for a few moments. It seemed to Cassidy that each person had gone inside themselves, lost in the seriousness of the situation they faced. Inside her belly Little Francis stirred. She thought of her desire to protect his life. She felt maternal toward all life on Earth. Perhaps Purlough was right; perhaps a woman full of new life was capable of understanding the rage and desperation Mother Earth must feel. Perhaps Earth has the right to expel mankind or radically reduce the population to bring things back into some kind of balance.

"What's a Caduceus?" David asked, breaking the long silence.

"Francis built a Caduceus to spiral spring water. It cured me of cancer."
Cassidy smiled at Francis.

David looked at Francis who was smiling. Cassidy knew what the smile meant. It was gratitude coupled with a good dose of smugness about his invention.

David let out a deep breath, "Wow, that explains a lot."

All three were quiet.

David started the car and asked, "Where to?"

"The hospital," Cassidy replied. "My water has broken. Sorry about your seat, David."

Chapter 25

Adam Halter strode around his condo in silk pajamas. His guards were down the hallway. It was his birthday. Gifts from high-placed Cartel members had arrived in a flood of tribute to his growing power. A tray of fruit and caviar had been delivered earlier.

Adam gloated that he had successfully unseated Purlough and was planning to take over the main office. Purlough's secretary had left crying after her first interaction with Adam. He was pleased; he had his own people and didn't trust her to keep his secrets.

Adam had expensive tastes. He disliked anything common. A beautifully handmade box of inlaid wood had just been delivered to his condo wrapped in birthday paper and topped with a bow made of hundred dollar bills. A small gift card said, "Wishing you every success, General Brigham".

Adam never suspected that the General's signature was forged. He had no way to know that beneath the lid was a firing mechanism that would end his life.

Adam held the box in his hand trying to open it. The top of the box was tightly held into place and his fingers could not pry it open. Taking a thin knife from a tray of fruit and caviar, Adam slipped the knife between the bottom and the lid of the box to pry it open.

The explosion was thunderous. It propelled Adam off his seat. His head was blown back, his face disintegrated, and his arms nearly detached from the body in shredded silk pajamas. He landed on the floor beneath a window that had been blown out.

Purlough had arranged the explosive device. He felt it a fitting end to his rival. The repercussions would be felt throughout the Cartel. No one had pushed a protégé forward with as much vigor as General Brigham. Adam's ego would not allow another to have a chance at power.

When Purlough was notified that his gift had been successful, he whispered to himself, "Thus ended the career of a prick."

Chapter 26

The waiting room was sparsely furnished. Vinyl seats with artificial wood backrests lined the pale green walls. Magazines on parenting and decorating had been read by countless nervous family members until pages fell from them in a helter skelter manner. Francis paced in front of a window that looked out across a small courtyard and faced a row of rooms in the next building. A pigeon made small circles on the window ledge across the way.

A nurse came out to talk to Francis and told him the C-section delivery was going to be difficult and asked him to wait there.

"Perhaps I should leave." David whispered to Francis.

"No, that's fine. Please, stay."

"Francis, you'll be fine. This is a private family moment. I feel in the way."

"David, I'll be better if I have someone to talk to."

An hour passed, but they talked very little. Francis continued to pace. David waited quietly.

Suddenly the doors swung open and the doctor came out.

"It was a difficult delivery, Mister Allenton." The doctor approached both of them, but addressed David. Francis raised his hand as if to signal the doctor that he was the father. At the same time, David pointed to Francis. The doctor murmured an apology for his mistake.

"Is she, are they, I mean, is everything, everybody all right?" Francis asked.

"Yes, as far as we can tell. We had a few tense moments. I won't make light of it. The baby was at risk, but everyone seems to be all right at the moment. Your wife is resting. I'll send a nurse soon to bring you in. We are going to do some blood tests on your new little girl."

"Girl? Did you say girl?" Francis asked.

"Why, yes. Didn't you know?" The doctor replied.

"No. We had anticipated a boy."

"She is a fine baby girl. We want to do a screen for antibodies. It is customary to do in all high risk pregnancies."

"I thought we planned for that."

"Yes, we did the proper prenatal care, but we want to look at the baby's antigens."

"Because?"

"We want to be certain that any produced antibodies do not attack the baby's red blood cells. Depending on when your wife passed her antibodies on to the baby, there may be a mild effect or a more serious problem."

"More serious?" Francis drew closer to the doctor.

"It is a routine set of tests. We just want to be certain. The neonatologist will give you the results." He turned and left abruptly.

David patted Francis on the back. "Well, congratulations, Daddy. I'm sure she will be fine."

"A girl?" Francis muttered. "Yes, thanks, David. I wasn't expecting a girl."

"Do you want me to wait around until you know something about the little one?" David asked.

Francis could see the kindness within him. He understood how Cassidy had liked him. He was a good man, given to fits of daring, but a good man.

"No. No, I imagine we can handle things from here. I'll call you, David and — thanks, David."

"Tell Cassy that I said, 'Good job!' "

David walked across the hall and the doors of the waiting elevator closed behind him.

A nurse in surgical scrubs came to the waiting room door. "Mr. Allenton?" She motioned for Francis to follow her. She had him wash with antibacterial soap and put on scrubs. He followed her like a dutiful child follows his mother in church. She pushed open a door and motioned him to enter.

Cassidy looked so tired resting on pillows and cradling a small, blanketed bundle, their baby.

Francis walked in quietly and touched Cassidy's cheek and then lightly touched the thin hair on the baby's head.

"We made a beautiful girl, Mama. There goes the name we had picked out."

"Yes. Not little Francis, but our little girl. There was a time I did wonder what we'd do if it wasn't a little boy. I thought about the name Destinee. What do you think, Francis? Do you like that?"

"Hmmm. Destinee Allenton. Yes, I like that." Francis laid his hand on Cassidy's shoulder, leaned over and smiling at his new daughter, whispered, "Hello, Destinee."

A nurse stood by the door. She spoke softly, "The doctor will be right with you. He wants to talk to both of you."

"Francis, hand me my glasses, will you. I must look a fright." Cassidy looked up.

With one hand she smoothed her hair down then took the glasses and pushed them on as the doctor walked in talking, "I'm the neonatologist. I want to talk to both of you about the results of the blood test." He was holding a long piece of paper in his hands.

"What's wrong?" Cassidy and Francis asked simultaneously.

"Nothing, but, I must say it is an unusual finding. We did the test and, well, it seems she has antibodies already. There are an unusual number of antibodies that are not attached to the blood cells. It is a highly unusual finding. Actually, we've been seeing these numbers here and there, randomly occurring, some children being born with highly developed immune systems. Advanced Immune Capacity, some are calling it."

"What does it mean?" Francis asked.

"It means she is naturally immune to most known diseases. We don't fully understand why this is happening, but some of the babies we have seen in the last year have highly developed immune systems. Normally, babies don't have immune systems at birth."

"Produced by what process?" Francis again asked.

"Perhaps it is the bone marrow, some of the specialists are suggesting an evolutionary development, kind of an adaptation or mutation, but the main result is she will be an extraordinarily healthy child. We are cautioning parents against the routine inoculations for childhood diseases as they are already protected. We think the mother is passing the immunity on to the child in some manner that we do not fully understand."

"I think I understand." Cassidy said slowly. "It's nature's way of insuring our survival. When the whole of humanity is beset by plagues and illnesses, a portion of humankind will survive. When the rest of us can no longer drink the water or breathe the air or when a great illness arises to decimate the human population and put us back into balance with the rest of nature, only some will survive. It's part of a plan. I see it now. It's beautiful and amazing at the same time."

"I'm sorry, Mr. and Mrs. Allenton, I need to go." The doctor had a puzzled look on his face as he left.

Francis pulled a chair over to sit next to Cassidy and Destinee.

Cassidy saw darkness in the future and, in the same instant, she saw a glimmer of hope. She didn't know exactly what it was that she felt when she looked at Destinee. Perhaps it was maternalism, perhaps something else, but she believed that Mother Earth had placed Destinee in their hands.

Chapter 27

The rest of the world and all other obligations were suspended as Cassidy and Francis pulled into a cave of preoccupation for several weeks after Destinee's birth. Francis focused the most on Destinee while Cassidy enjoyed watching his evolution into fatherhood. He talked about feelings emerging from unknown places for his child. He explained to Cassidy that he'd never been exposed to paternalism. His father was absent during most of childhood and his mother tried to fill the vacuum. He thought that a degree of his social clumsiness came from not having a father figure.

Now he found himself doting on Destinee, amazed at this child made by his love for Cassidy. He said his role as a father felt natural and comfortable. If Destinee made sounds and faces, they were interpreted by Francis as confirmation of her brightness. If she fussed, Francis sprung into action to make certain that nothing was disturbing her. He often checked on her when she was sleeping to make sure she was breathing or just to check her covers.

Cassidy took motherhood more in stride. She had a deep maternal love and easily bonded to her daughter, but nursing education had given her a clinical detachment from the noises and discomforts of a baby. They were to be expected. Sometimes she even felt she was less patient as a parent than Francis. She knew, however, that some of her impatience was her skin rash that continued to itch and burn night and day. The red blotches emerged and no amount of intervention from soothing creams or oatmeal baths brought relief. She found the continually emerging sensitivities maddening.

"Get the phone, will you?" Cassidy called to Francis. "I'm trying to get Destinee to nurse. Maybe this time we won't have to supplement with a bottle."

"Okay — hello!" Francis said picking up the phone.

"Francis?"

"You got me."

"This is Maurice."

"Well, old boy, it's been a while. I thought you were prohibited from calling me."

"Have you been following the news in the Gulf?"

"No, to tell you the truth."

"The research group has been putting out news releases about the dead zone."

"And?"

"And they have been reporting a reversal."

"We have been pretty busy of late with the baby and all."

"Yes. Excuse me. I should have said something, of course, you have a new little one. Congratulations."

"That's fine, Maurice, we're fine."

Maurice was silent for a moment.

Francis was distracted by Destinee's crying.

Cassidy yelled, "Who is it, Francis?"

Covering the mouthpiece, Francis yelled back, "Maurice."

"Tell him I said hello, Bonjour, I mean." Cassidy yelled above the crying.

At the same time, Maurice spoke, "Francis, it's the containment."

Francis suddenly gave Maurice his full attention. "What did you say?"

"It was breached — the containment. Purposefully, I might add, by the man who was looking for you."

"How do you know it was him?"

"Surveillance footage on the platform."

"Son of a bitch. He needs to be held accountable for this."

"Don't worry, he has been! He's dead. Blown up by a bomb on his birthday."

"No shit?"

"No shit!"

Cassidy walked from the kitchen into the living room. Destinee was whimpering and fussing on Cassidy's shoulder.

"What's he saying?" she whispered.

"Just a minute, Maurice." Putting his hand over the phone again, "Nothing, Cass."

Cassidy shot back, "Francis, are you telling me that Maurice called from France to say nothing?"

Francis knew Cassidy would be upset if he told her that Maurice had details about the Gulf waters being purposefully used to reverse the Dead Zones. He felt she had enough with a new baby to worry about plus her unrelenting skin irritations.

"Cassidy, he heard about the baby."

"That's sweet of him. Now, what is he really saying? Was it part of the project you worked on?"

"Yes."

"Why? What happened?"

"Just the containment. Maurice says there are press releases about a reversal."

"So it was intentionally released in the Gulf?"

"I didn't say that."

Cassidy had been shaking a bottle of formula. She began to shake it more vigorously. "God Damn liars. What have they done now?"

"Now, Cass, we knew the containment wasn't working." He released his hand and spoke into the phone, "I'm sorry, Maurice — "

Cassidy had not drawn a breath, "Francis, I can tell Maurice knows a lot more than we do. Let me talk to him." She held out her hand for the phone.

"Cassidy, they said not to get too angry."

"I am not angry." She said pointing the nipple end of the bottle at him. "Give me the fucking phone. I want to know what they have done."

Francis spoke into the phone, "Maurice, are you still there?"

"Yes."

"She wants to talk to you."

"I have to run."

"I wouldn't do that if I were you." Francis warned.

"Run?"

"Yes."

Francis handed her the phone.

"Feed her, will you?" Cassidy lowered Destinee to his lap and handed him the bottle.

"Maurice?" she said into the phone.

"Yes, Madame Allenton, I hear things are going well for you."

"Not really. I have a rash that puts me on fire. I can't sleep at night."

"I am most sorry to hear that."

"Tell me why you called."

"To wish you well."

"Maurice, you do not lie very well. What is this with the containment?"

"It's nothing. Really."

"Nothing enough to call from France?"

"Well, a little something."

"I am aware by talking to Francis that there might be containment issues. Has stellar water been released in the Gulf?"

"It's not certain."

"Meaning that it isn't being released for the public?"

"You know much, Madame Allenton."

"How was it done?"

"A man, an associate of the Water Cartel was responsible. He was a wild card. He was the man that came to France to get rid of Francis. I didn't like him. No matter, he is with eternity now."

"Have there been changes? I mean, have there been alterations in the sea life?"

"Yes."

"Mutations?"

"Yes."

"Adaptation or mutations"

"A difficult distinction, Madame Allenton."

"Are the changes getting out of hand?"

"As you would anticipate, Mother Nature is responding by making changes of her own."

"It's out of control. Isn't it?"

"Yes. We are seeing changes. The plankton are changing and growing, fed by the algae blooms in the dead zones. We are seeing a Cambrian level of change in the microscopic sea life."

"Explosive development?"

"Yes. They are developing rapidly, evolving if you will or mutating, depending on your perspective. The sea is making changes to accommodate these alterations. Early indications are that the reefs are under threat. The movements of the radiolaria are wider than anticipated. Computer models of the spread have suggested a world wide expansion in as few as twenty months."

"What are they predicting for the reefs?"

"Collapse. Total Collapse."

"I don't need to tell you, if the reefs collapse the entire eco system of the oceans will change, perhaps die."

"I understand. I need help. My own people are busy marketing the Dead Zone Solution, micro organisms that cleanse the sea. They are not telling the story of the consequences to the oceans. Sad thing, it is true. They are cleaning up the dead zones, but they will eventually kill the reef systems unless something happens. Something quick."

"You want us to become involved."

"Yes. I can't really say anything. Not to the public."

"You must."

"I cannot. The people in the project are dangerous. That kind of money is always attached to danger. Doctor Allenton is being funded to examine the Gulf area. You have contacts that matter. I can't really get involved."

"You are. We all are. Don't you see? Gaia is responding to the interventions. A problem is presented to the public wrapped in a false, dangerous solution and Mother Earth must respond. It's how the natural system is hard wired. The very nature of evolution is to adapt. When you add this to the mix, the system automatically reacts and produces a counter reaction."

"It is essential that we know the consequences to the reefs. These models may be wrong."

"Maurice, is there no one within your system?"

"There is one man. He is deathly sick. Word has it he will give a sympathetic ear."

"Purlough?"

"You know this man. Good."

"I'll talk to Francis. Maurice, I want to thank you."

"For?"

"Caring about the Earth. Not many do."

"I think it is the proper thing to do."

"Thank you, Maurice. We will get back to you."

Chapter 28

The phone rang in Alford Purlough's bedroom. He stirred reluctantly from a deep sleep and reached for it. The phone fell to the floor. Rolling on his side and sliding half on and half off the bed, he groaned and he grabbed it. Pulling himself up, taking a breath, he spoke, "Purlough."

"It has arrived." The man said. "The container has been unloaded. It is in a warehouse now. What are your instructions?"

"I have an address in New Orleans for you. I'll have to confirm. Give me a day or so."

"There has been some damage to the crate."

"That is an unacceptable event."

"None the less."

"The cargo inside that crate is essential for my survival."

"I am aware."

"You are talking strangely. Is there something else going on?"

"A man has offered a large sum for the crate. A sum that is tempting."

"You had best not even entertain that as a possibility."

"This man is with your own organization. A man of some power I should say."

"The General?"

"As I said, a most generous man."

"Did he say why he wanted it?"

"Because you did."

"What are your plans?"

"You and I go back a long way, but a man has to look to his future. I understand you are gravely ill and without the power you once had."

"I remain a powerful man. Not a man to cross."

"Don't threaten me, Purlough. It's beneath you."

"Don't dance with me. What do you want?"

"Twice the fee he offered."

"I don't know. Now I'm not sure it's worth — ."

"There is something else as well. Information."

"About?"

"A carpet cleaning plan I know of."

"I see."

"Yes. The generous man has ordered some carpet cleaning. I know the men in that company. They inform me of things from time to time."

"Then I might be willing to pay your price. Can you ask your associates to alter their agreement with the General?"

"It is most difficult. It might be possible."

"Can we come to an agreement then?"

"Perhaps we can."

"So, the crate and the cancellation of the cleaning."

"The cancellation of the cleaning might be a problem."

"I know the company. I have worked with them before."

"So you know they have a reputation for completing their assignments. It will take substantial financial incentives to sway them."

"I will supply that. We have an agreement then?"

"We do."

"I shall have the address for the crate delivery to you before the day is out."

"I will have details about the fee when next we talk."

Purlough sank back in his pillows. He knew the day would come when the Cartel would attempt to silence him. It was the fate of the wicked, when weak, to be killed by the wild pack. He had been the first to act, removing Adam on his own initiative. He knew it was risky, but he knew that the only way to gain retribution for the death of his granddaughter was to act first. He knew as well that the General would know. No one else within the Cartel would dare to make such a move. He chided himself that his illness had slowed his thinking. He should have taken the General and Adam with the same blow, but Adam was the one he most wanted to hurt. Now he realized that the General would find another protégé.

Purlough suspected the illness that robbed his strength might be part of a plan to kill him. Making him weak and removing his power would be the first logical step.

They hadn't counted on the death of his granddaughter, or perhaps they had. Perhaps they targeted her school and her classroom. The Cartel had grown dark with greed and power, darker than it had ever been.

Purlough had a plan, motivated by revenge, regret and anger. He wanted to expose the Cartel, bring them down the way they had tried to bring him down. He wanted to make them pay for his granddaughter's death. He wanted to put something in the plus column of his life. He had a lot of time to think. He wondered if it wasn't the wish of all dying people, to put something down in the book of life that was positive to erase or balance the other deeds of their lives. Whatever the plan, he wanted to make the Cartel suffer like he was suffering.

The funding of Francis, David and their efforts toward watching the Gulf had been the first step. The removal of Adam came next. The elimination of the General was ambitious, even for a man of power like himself. He lay in bed, day after day, pushing his mind to formulate a plan. Death stalked him. He gained a glimpse of it in the mirror: his thin, rakish body and his dark, deep set eyes. He was aware of his shaking arms and loss of appetite, but determined that death would be cheated, day by day, minute by minute, until he had his way with life. Isolated and alone, there was no one he could talk to. No one shared his glee about the revenge taken. No one knew his inner thoughts.

During his planning process, he had invented a friendship with Cassidy. Not because she cared for him, but because she cared deeply about life. He let his mind go to his own funeral and imaged Cassidy standing near his corpse, touching his hand and whispering she was sorry. Sorry for his suffering. Sorry for his losses. Sorry for his choices. Tears would form in her eyes. Tears of precious water that would heal him of his self-loathing as they fell upon his hand. Now in life, he allowed his own tears to flow while he replayed his fantasy like a movie in his mind.

Chapter 29

Francis and Cassidy heard a knock at the front door. They were discussing the call from Maurice. Cassidy pulled herself up from sitting with her legs crossed beneath her torso. After almost a year, she was pleased to once again sit in her favorite position.

She opened the door with a wide sweep of her arms and bid David to enter.

"You're spunky." David observed.

Cassidy observed that his smile was tense and his eyes purposeful, but responded to his comment, "Getting my body back from pregnancy ransom."

David looked around, "Francis here?"

"Yes. After you rang the doorbell, he thought he heard Destinee waking up. Come on in. You look worried." Cassidy searched his eyes. She remembered that look with the deep furrows above his eyes as he worked on a problem.

"The back waters are getting weird."

"Weird?" Francis came around the corner holding Destinee cradled in his right arm. She was reaching her arms into the air as if trying to catch something.

"Yeah. Hi there, baby!" David put out his finger to Destinee who grasped it and made a gurgle noise. "Weird. I don't know. Just something I feel. The water's gone all different out at the house."

Cassidy and Francis looked at each other.

"What?" David asked.

Francis responded, "We just had a call from Maurice."

"And?"

"He thinks there's a problem. Not only in the Gulf but maybe world wide."

"Problem?" David asked looking into Cassidy's eyes. Did he remember how vulnerable she was to his intense, direct gaze?

"Yes." She said. "It's possible some new mutation has occurred secondary to the introduction of stellar water into the Gulf. It was part of a clean up process, micro organisms eating the algae."

"Stellar water? You mean that project Francis was on?"

"One and the same." Francis said. "Maurice called to say their projection models on the computers indicate a possible mutation with consequent reaction that may cause the reefs to collapse."

Cassidy took Destinee from Francis and rocked her back and forth in front of her.

David looked at Francis, "Man, they are fragile enough already. What's being done?"

"Nothing." Cassidy interjected shaking her head back and forth. Destinee grabbed a fistful of her mommy's golden hair moving past her. Cassidy had to bend her head toward the tiny hand and pull the hair from her grip. She made a face as she said, "Ouch!".

Francis and Cassidy were momentarily distracted, but David was not, "Why did he call?

Francis immediately responded, "He's worried. He can't say anything as an insider. The 'powers that be' are marketing the mutation as a cleaning agent for the dead zones. He's in too deep to stop the process, he had no idea that the examination of the stellar water would lead to this. He's not the first to be duped by the Cartel. He called because the computer models project major collapses."

"Mother's reacting!" David turned to Cassidy gesturing as if needing confirmation yet hoping he was wrong. "I'm right, aren't I, Cassy? Oh, man."

"Yes. She's producing changes to counteract the mutations."

"Escalation of consequence. Don't they know anything? One change leads to another, leads to another. What's his computer model say?"

"Reef collapse, global changes." Francis said. "The mutations are spreading fast. Picked up by winds, tides, current and who knows what, the changes are beginning to move past the Gulf."

"My God. Don't they know what they started?"

"Profits, my friend, profits drive them." As she spoke Cassidy held Destinee very still.

"That eco system is already stressed by pollution, contaminants, temperature changes, extinctions. If the seas die, we die. When will they get it?" David moaned.

"When the Oceans are dead, when the last whale is dead, we are next. When Mother stands up and starts kicking our butts off this planet, maybe then they will get it. Maybe not." She moved toward David, "David, we can't — "

He interrupted her, "We have to act." He shook his head like someone does looking at a meaningless, fatal accident that might have been avoided, then added, "Like Purlough said. We have to act. We have to sound the alarm." He turned and began pacing, "We got to get this to the news, today."

"They don't really care, David." Cassidy said. "We have tried for three generations to tell the world, but it falls on deaf ears."

"We have never had a crisis like this looming." Francis joined in watching David pace. "If the reefs collapse, then they will see what's coming."

Cassidy raised her hand as if to signal a mute protest to the idea that calamity brings clarity. "Why would they see anything if the reefs collapse? We have had extreme dependency on oil with no sense of what's happening. We have had global warming. We have had extinctions of entire eco systems. We have justified war for the sake of oil and not risked a single life for the planet. We have had crisis after crisis and always the hope that technology or some invention will save us. For all our advances, we are just as dependent upon Mother Earth as we were when we crawled from the sea. The sea is the source of all of us, and when we kill the sea, we truly begin the end of all things. Mother must know. She is beginning to make preparations."

"What's their official position? I mean, what's being said in the news?" David asked Francis.

"I don't know. Most likely they will say the mutations occurred naturally as a consequence of tritium or some other substance occurring in the water. I am sure they will distance themselves from the release. Probably they will say confidently that it is a natural occurrence."

"Tritium doesn't occur naturally, does it?" David asked standing still watching Francis.

"Well, actually, yes it does, but less than one percent of tritium occurs naturally through the interaction of cosmic rays with molecules of certain elements in the upper atmosphere. Only trace amounts ever end up in the oceans. They cannot be blamed for the alteration of entire ecosystems." Francis had shifted into his professorial lecture mode. The shift was smooth as if some switch in his memory was silently thrown and stored information was unlocked.

"So if it is in greater amounts, it causes mutation." Cassidy stated.

"I'm afraid so. Tritium is mutagenic. It can be taken into the body by inhalation, absorption through the skin or ingestion. Consider ingestion, it gets into the body system when the water that carries it is absorbed from the gastrointestinal tract and mixed with the total body water. It soon begins to corrupt the tissues as they are comprised mostly of water.

"Tritium can harm living organisms by emitting beta particles, which can break chemical bonds and damage living cells, particularly through damage to DNA molecules. Damage to the DNA of sperm or egg cells can result in damage to future generations. These damages result in mutations. The most sensitive populations to tritium are fetuses, young children and women of childbearing age."

"I didn't exactly understand how it would do damage," David interrupted, "but the mutations, that's why we went to Canada years ago to protest the release of tritium from the nuclear electricity plants."

"Yes, David, that was important since food or animal products raised near nuclear generating stations may be a significant source of organically bound tritium. Once animals or plants ingest the tritium through food or water, they have radioactive elements in their tissues. When humans ingest the food or animal products, they suffer severe health problems and genetic mutations. What complicates all this is that tritium mimics normal hydrogen in water making that water indistinguishable from safe water."

"Mutations? So we have tritium causing mutations in humans — " Cassidy stopped as if she were thinking aloud.

"Yes. Go on." Francis said. He looked at David, then waited.

"Would you say that mutations can be both positive and negative? Adaptations that make a certain group within a species more resistant to disease, for instance, could be a positive adaptation. Therefore, not every mutation is a negative event?"

"No. Some mutations are beneficial."

"Would you say that in one context mutations are evolutionary?"

"Certainly."

David continued to watch them. They were going back and forth. Cassidy asked questions as if she were anticipating Francis' scientific answers. Francis waited for her to lead.

"So, changes may be taking place, seen and unseen, as a consequence to the change in the sea?" Cassidy asked.

"Yes."

"If Mother had anticipated or knew to react, would it be likely that mutations would be taking place?"

"If she were aware." Francis clearly emphasized the "if" and Cassidy knew he did that to keep her from running full force forward with her idea.

"Francis, she is aware. She knows what is happening. There is no 'if' to it. Now, let me ask you this: if a species is preparing to alter, are there signs in the species before the alteration?"

"Cass, that is a difficult question. In some instances, yes, there are signs of change. One generation will make a partial adaptation, sometimes even appearing sick or weak and their offspring will be born with the mutation or adaptation."

"So, if the parents have a problem, sometimes it is an indication that the offspring will be changed in some way?"

"Yes, in some cases, that is true. The alterations in the parents prepare the way for genetic changes in the offspring."

"Like a weakness or some alteration in pigmentation, something like that?"

"Yes. Why?"

"This damn rash. The strong spread of multiple chemical sensitivity all over the world and, in particular, people near the coast, it's Mother's way of preparing a new generation to be ready. The parents have a weakness, changes in skin. The skin is the largest organ of the body. It makes sense, doesn't it? If we are going to change in a way to survive what is coming, if Mother wants some of us to be strong and survive, then there are alterations in the parents to assure mutations, and then, positive mutations in our children so they will survive. Mother will not exterminate us. She will change us perhaps, reduce our numbers significantly, but she will not exterminate us. She has too much invested in us. Even if we are reaping havoc on the Earth, She has spent too much evolutionary energy on us to just do away with us. She will find a way to make us adapt and survive."

"Are you saying that Destinee is an adaptation?" Francis looked at their daughter asleep in Cassidy's arms.

"An evolution, like a lot of the children the doctor told us about. They have extreme immunity and it is unexplained. Children don't have immunity right away. They develop antibodies when they are exposed to disease or have the potential in their blood, but they are not born with the immunities. Destinee and many other babies are now being born with this super immunity. It's Mother's way. I'm sure of it. She knows what's coming."

David listened to all of this and, at one point, raised his hand like a young boy in grade school. He sat with his hand up, waiting for them to acknowledge him as they went back and forth. Finally, Francis and Cassidy looked at him. He smiled a boyish grin, his hand in the air like a student that knows the answer to the teacher's question.

"Yes, David?" they said almost in unison.

"I know, we know, but so few others get it. The reefs will die. The oceans will change. The world will seem on the edge of collapse. Perhaps millions of humans will die as a consequence of the changes that have begun, but Mother will prevail. I'm right! I know I'm right. In the end, when we have done everything we can possibly do to ruin her, Mother will prevail. It's beautiful man, beautiful."

Francis and Cassidy listened to David but were looking at Destinee. After David finished, Francis spoke, "We must do what we can to alert others. We must sound the warning." He took Destinee in his arms. "We owe it to the Earth and to the children to use all we have to bring healing."

About the Author

Dennis Edwards received his PhD and Masters of Social Work from the University of Illinois. His formal career spanned college administration, counseling, teaching, consulting and grant writing. In those settings he wrote a wide variety of newspaper and periodical articles and authored chapters in social work textbooks. In 2005 his novel, *The Caduceus*, the first in a trilogy focused on global water issues, was enthusiastically received by readers. His fiction is based on extensive research of historical events and current environmental issues.

In addition to fiction, Edwards writes poetry, draws cartoons, and oil paints. He serves on the Board of Directors for the Ozarks Writer's League and was published in their first anthology, *Echoes of the Ozarks. Volume 1*. Dennis has a passionate commitment to the preservation of the natural environment where he lives and fly fishes in the Ozarks.